DOUBLE CROSS

A TOM SHEPARD REDACTED MISSION FILE

PHILLIP JORDAN

FIVE FOUR PUBLISHING

Get Exclusive Material

GET EXCLUSIVE NEWS AND UPDATES FROM THE AUTHOR

Thank-you for choosing to read this book.

Sign-up for more details about my life growing up on the same streets as Tom Shepard and get an exclusive e-book containing an in-depth interview and a selection of True Crime stories about the flawed but fabulous city that inspired me to write, *all for free.*

Details can be found at the end of **DOUBLE CROSS.**

Prologue

The Black Sea Coast

The narrow side street was free of traffic just as the delivery driver expected given the lateness of the hour, and he had no problems manoeuvring the liveried Mercedes Sprinter van through a three-point turn and reversing down a sloping concrete ramp that led to a strip of sandy beach. The building that was his point of reference lay across the street.

The Thracian Grand Palace Hotel overlooked the narrow road and the sea beyond, and as the driver opened his door, the humidity of the evening washed over him. The whirr of the hotel's air conditioning units and the soft lap of water onto the shore ten metres away offered a soporific serenade compared to the raucous beat of electronic dance music that drifted from the beach bars and nightclubs half a kilometre further along the sandy cove.

The ancient Bulgarian seaside town of Sozopol jutted out into the now dark waters of the Black Sea. The popular tourist destination nestled on a crescent of dramatic rocky coastline equidistant from the borders of Turkey to the south and Romania to the north.

Shuffling to the back of the vehicle, the driver unlatched the rear shutter which was emblazoned with the Zora commercial laundry logo and slid it half open, exposing a cargo compartment that contained the carcasses of six large, heavy-duty polyester laundry sacks. He turned and sauntered down the rutted concrete access ramp. Feet shod in cheap flip-flops sank into the soft sand and he pulled a pack of Gorna Djumaya cigarettes from the pocket of his torn skinny jeans, teasing one out with his teeth and sparking it up with a plastic disposable lighter. As he inhaled the strong tobacco smoke, he scratched his stomach through a black string vest and surveyed the moonlight on the rolling waves crashing against the sand. It was as peaceful a spot for a five-minute break as could be hoped if you were in the middle of a manic night shift distributing laundry around the resort's exclusive hotels and private seafront villas.

He slowly blew out a long stream of smoke, the mild sea breeze snatching it away from his face and he whistled the first few bars of 'Danny Boy'.

Away to his right, the tide surged against rocky man-made groynes, a sudden crash and splash of waves pounding home lifted foam and saltwater into the air.

As he took another drag of the cigarette, the next melodic phrase of 'The Londonderry Air' that lent the popular Irish ballad its tune whistled back.

The driver flicked his cigarette into the sand and turned to face the shadows melting out from the lee of the robust coastal defence.

"Nice outfit, Gash. You going for the full euro sex-pest look?"

"It might have to stay," said the driver, running a hand

over his slicked back, collar-length hair and then licking his lips lasciviously and stroking his handlebar moustache, he added. "Your sister said she loves it."

"Christ, Gash, have you seen Token's sister?" A second figure hustled across the sand behind the first, Sergeant Mark Mills giving the man a playful thump on the arm as he passed. Both men carried a long canvas bag in one hand and each had a large pack slung across their opposite shoulder.

Corporal Andy 'Token' Moore gave a lopsided grin as he greeted his comrade, Corporal Gareth 'Gash' Day, and slung first the bag and then the pack into the rear of the Sprinter to accompany those of Mills.

Token's nickname had been bestowed by his colleagues as he was the only man in their small unit of green army descent. His route into the elite UK Special Forces unit identified as Task Force Trident had started in the Parachute Regiment before his selection into the Special Air Service (SAS). As Moore had fallen from the sky Mills, Gash and the team commander, Captain Tom Shepard had risen from the sea, all three men having initially earned their coveted green berets on completion of Royal Marine commando training at Lympstone in Devon before enduring their own torturous selection programme to finally become badged in the Royal Navy's elite Special Boat Service (SBS).

"Our Nikki would snap you in half if she heard you say that," said Token, turning to face Gash, who had a wistful smile on his face as he kicked sand from his flip-flops.

"Aye, but a way to go," he said, picturing the raven-haired beauty who also happened to be reigning UK judo champion.

"All aboard," said Mills, scanning the quiet street. "Clock's ticking and we don't want to be keeping the boss waiting when we've got a whale to land."

The fisherman cut his outboard and allowed the small fishing vessel to slice through the black water towards the shore. The waves slapping against the fibreglass hull were the only sound in the gloom of the late evening save the occasional screech of a hungry gull hoping to claim a morsel of discarded catch.

The sea was calm and the evening humid, although the light westerly pushing the boat towards the sandy beach was just enough to cause the sweat of the working day to cool on the skin and the fisherman pulled his hood up over a baseball cap that sat low on his brow to ward off the chilling effect. His eyes scanned the shoreline to where several other sixteen footers lined the sand, the boats already tied up and empty of catch and crew.

The beach extended back to a band of thick marine grasses that rose up an incline and bordered a seafront faced by the brightly lit windows of the overlooking mansions and the exclusive villas which were set apart to maintain privacy from each other and from the public by means of shuttered gates or, in the instance of the one which drew his eye, a guardhouse with a complement of dour-looking guardians.

As a soft sandbar arrested the boat's momentum, a set of headlamps swept around a bend on the road beyond the beach, the vehicle's twin headlamps lancing across the darkened sand as the driver negotiated the corner, proceeding along the shore road to light up the gatehouse and drawing the attention of the men inside. They stepped out onto the pavement, the car lights flashing as it closed, and then drew to a stop. The fisherman didn't need to be able to read the liveried words on the side of the Kia Ceed. The white and blue colour scheme and roof-mounted light bar was a dead giveaway that the local police were doing the rounds.

Under the glow of street lights, he could see the bulk of pistols tucked into the gate guards' trousers as they leaned into the police car, but neither that nor the presence of the local authorities fazed him. He was there to get a job done, one that could have been completed months ago but for the technicalities and legalities of international diplomacy and the hand wringing of those politicians charged with authorising incursions inside the borders of supposedly friendly nations.

Leaping over the bulwark, the fisherman splashed into knee-high water. Grabbing a thick rope tied to the prow, he dragged the small boat onto the sand, bringing it to rest at a point well away from the men on the road above. Steadying the craft on several buoys, he leaned in to haul a large lobster pot up onto the gunwale, tugging the drawstring that narrowed the pot's neck and pulling out not the day's catch but a black polyurethane waterproof sack.

Dropping to his haunches in the lee of the boat, he dug into the bag, extracting a small earpiece and throat mic attached to a secure SELEX comms unit. Fitting the apparatus with proficient speed, he then thumbed the power switch and channel selector, receiving a blip of connectivity and a warbled signal acquisition tone. Online and able to communicate, he finally retrieved the last item from the bag, a suppressed Heckler and Koch USP 9 pistol.

"Six-two, this is Neptune. How copy?" he said, observing the men on the roadside who continued their conversation oblivious to his presence, the Kia quietly pumping a plume of exhaust fumes into the night air.

"Neptune, loud and clear. ETA two mikes."

"Be advised local presence at the target site. Standby." Neptune listened to the clipped affirmative from the inbound team before unzipping his jacket and retrieving a burlap duffel bag from inside the boat. Leaving the shelter of the hull, he walked across the beach to a set of wooden steps that led up to the road. He took his time, striding confidently with his senses totally focused on the chatter ahead.

"Six-two, target in twenty."

Captain Tom Shepard acknowledged the report with a double click of his mic.

Up ahead one of the guards was smoking, the other let out a bark of laughter and then rapped the roof of the police car with a big fist.

A chorus of affable chuckles and goodbyes rang out and then the Kia crunched into gear and drove off. The two guards traded words and although the conversation was lost to the sound of the waves on the beach, their body language broadcast it was about one of the men in the car.

As the two men began to return to their post they caught sight of the shambling figure and turned to observe the weary fisherman as he approached.

"*Dobar den*," said the larger of the two men in greeting as he had every night for the last two weeks. His big head dipped in a nod to tap his square chin against a broad chest. Shepard returned the nod, closing the gap a little quicker as he heard the sound of a vehicle closing from behind him.

The second guard flicked his cigarette into the road where it exploded in a shower of sparks, and as he blew out his last breath the two men locked eyes. A second later the fisherman was silhouetted by the headlights of an approaching van.

The guard raised a hand to shield his eyes from the glare of a full beam and then the rasp of the vehicle's brakes masked the double cough of the suppressed pistol.

The first guard twitched in surprise, reaching up to touch his face, confusion etched on his brow at the sudden wet spit smearing his cheek.

Dropping the burlap duffel bag to the ground, Shepard moved with the speed and agility of a striking shark.

The burly Bulgarian was halfway through his turn, a question for his partner dying on his lips and his eyes bulging at the scene that had unfolded four paces away. His hand dropped to tug at the FN five-seven semi-automatic tucked into the waistband of his chinos.

Covering the ground quicker than the guard could draw, Shepard snapped his own pistol on target and sent a round into the centre of the big man's chest from point-blank range, the impact rocked the guard back on his heels and blasted the breath from his ruptured lungs. Before his brain had time to process the pain, two more rounds had slammed home on either side of the first and his body crumpled to the pavement.

The van stopped and the back doors swung open.

"Jamming is active, and the clock has started," said Mark Mills, leaping from the vehicle and dragging out one of the large laundry sacks.

Shepard nodded his understanding, glancing at the luminous index and numbers of his diver's watch and making note. His observations of the villa and the police patrol over the last weeks gave them a solid time frame in which to act, and it was now T-minus thirty-seven minutes until the patrol came past on its next sweep.

He grabbed the dead guard's feet and helped Mills manoeuvre the body into the laundry sack. To their right Token and Gash were bagging the other dead guard and within twenty seconds it was as if the first line of Khalid Alfredi's defence had never existed.

Khalid Alfredi rolled over in the king-size bed and swept the sheet from his naked body. Reaching out to touch the screen of the iPhone laying on the bedside cabinet, he noted the time. It was late but not the middle of the night, as he had thought.

The air in the room was still and humid but temperature aside he was unsettled and sleep had been fleeting even after the evening's exertions with the acrobatic Slovenian escort, and now he was awake, thoughts of drifting back over were far from his mind.

As he stood up, the woman in the bed stirred, coiling herself in the sheets as the Egyptian padded naked to his laptop which sat on a glass and driftwood desk overlooking the expansive gardens and the raven black blur of the sea and horizon beyond.

Lifting the MacBook's lid he inputted a twenty digit alphanumeric passcode from memory. He waited for the VPN programme to run before launching an encrypted connection to a second host server, this prompting him for a further authentication code, and he once again entered a string of digits and then finally, he was connected to his cryptocurrency exchange.

Scanning the markets, a wry smile crossed his face when he noted there was blood in the water and several of the popular currencies had lost ground in the last hours, leaving bargains to be snapped up as investors dumped their holdings in panic.

The fledgling cryptocurrency markets were the Wild West of financial investment, swinging from glorious highs to cruel lows, but for Alfredi they offered something else; a secure, anonymous and lucrative way to channel his illicit wealth, one that was far from the tendrils of governments and the manipulation of banking institutions and law enforcement and, more importantly, invisible to the eyes of those he worked for.

The Egyptian clicked open a window and consulted a transfer of fiat currencies which made up the bulk of three million US dollars, payment for his most recent services and funds to secure another batch of volunteers and the purchase of munitions, transport and storage necessary for the next wave of their operations.

Alfredi clicked through several more accounts, depositing funds which would, in turn, be used to pay his chain of suppliers, facilitators and those local officials who aided his operations where routes through red tape and official channels needed to be expedited or struck from the record. Finally, he selected an account to which only he had access, smiling at the coffers of bitcoin and similar untraceable wealth which he had amassed over the previous two years.

Wiping a bead of sweat from his upper lip, he selected a healthy proportion of his benefactor's funds and redirected them to his personal holdings, converting the material currency to ethereal crypto coins. Skimming the cream was a huge risk given the people he was working for, however, he was ambivalent. He believed that in this game you needed a buffer, and his would not just be one that could get him out of trouble fast, it would also be large enough to allow him to disappear forever. The Egyptian did not plan to hide out in squalor if either the authorities or the cartels and warlords came searching for him. He intended to be far from reach and very well protected.

The glow of the laptop screen lit up his face, the sum displayed was a fantastical amount, and he pondered for a moment what the young man who had grown up in Cairo's sprawling Ezbet El Haggana slums would say if he could see his future self. The Egyptian's path over the intervening years had been precipitous, frequently courting death and torture since the overthrow of the Mubarak regime, an event which may not have seen prosperity returned to the people of his country, but one which had presented him with opportunity and enough reward to elevate himself to the gilded position he now enjoyed.

Satisfied with his work and accepting the notifications his trades had been successful, he closed the MacBook's lid and walked to a drinks trolley which was set to the right of the balcony doors. He picked up a bottle of spring water and cracked the seal, feeling a rivulet of sweat break free from the nape of his neck and roll down his back and, for the first time since waking, he realised the hum of the suite's air-con was absent.

He took a swig of the tepid water and walked across to the thermostat, dropping the plastic cover flap and prodding the temperature control key.

Nothing happened.

He frowned, retracing his steps to his desk where he tried the switch to illuminate the black and copper banker's lamp and again he was rewarded with no success.

As Alfredi looked out of the full-length windows at the adjoining properties and the illumination of the beachfront bars and clubs, the MacBook warbled a low battery warning. His eyes settled on the charging station, and the absence of power.

Despite the humidity, he shivered and tendrils of anxiety slipped around his stomach.

He started as the door to the suite opened.

Silhouetted in the doorway, pistol in hand, stood his head of personal security, Ramzy Joumaa. The big Jordanian was unfazed at seeing his charge standing naked by the windows.

"The power is out," said Alfredi, which Joumaa confirmed with a sharp nod.

"It's not the circuit breaker, Khalid. We have to go." He jerked his head to indicate they should leave the suite immediately.

As he moved across to the dresser, Khalid Alfredi for the first time in a long time felt as though a noose had begun to slip around his throat.

"X-ray, this is Trident Six-one. Sit-rep, waypoint secure. Confirm green?" said Shepard into his secure SELEX.

The comms blipped in advance of the order to proceed with the mission.

"Six-one. X-ray. Green confirmed. Standby. Midnight in three… two… one…"

Shepard watched the interior light in the guardhouse blink out as a secondary team cut power to the villa from the cable control cabinets several blocks away, rendering the complex's phones, internet and CCTV useless.

"Six-one, confirm midnight. Executing."

Shepard and the Task Force Trident team had been keeping Khalid Alfredi under surveillance for coming on six weeks. Prior to that, Alfredi had been identified and tracked by their colleagues in Task Force Falcon.

Interest in the Egyptian had been piqued when he was identified as the facilitator of an innocuous shipment of agricultural chemicals from Tunis to the Syrian port of Latakia. The spotlight falling firmly on him after Shepard, who was on a mission to secure an intelligence asset with evidence of war crimes, had joined forces with a group of ragtag Syrian rebels desperate to break the stranglehold of Pro-Government and Russian forces undertaking a brutal offensive against the north-west city of Maghrabad.

The unlikely group had stumbled on a stockpile of weaponised warheads and then faced off against the forces of a rogue Russian colonel who planned to use them against the rebels and their western alliance partners. Shepard eventually secured both his asset and vital intelligence identifying the chemical weapons route into the country whilst achieving a narrow victory over the Russian in a vicious hand to hand battle during the flight to safety. The wounds of that mission had healed with a few additional scars as the only visible reminder.

Stooping to pick up the discarded duffel bag, Shepard retrieved his suppressed Colt C8 CQB Carbine from inside, dropping out the magazine to pre-check the rounds and then slipping the weapon's three-point sling over his head. He let the short rifle hang free and entered the villa's guardhouse, thumbing the release switch for the tall, black gates which began to quietly open on greased runners.

Gash reversed the laundry van onto the paved drive, the area shielded from the main villa by geography and a swathe of manicured shrubs and tall palms.

In the weeks leading up to the night's offensive, Falcon's observations were at first passive, limited to tracking Alfredi's movements electronically; monitoring his passport and those of his assumed identities and tracing the facilitator's credit card, phone and internet usage by means of spyware surreptitiously installed on the man's various devices.

The surveillance had escalated to more traditional methods when twenty civilians died and a further thirty were seriously injured in a suicide bomb attack on a hotel in the Turkish resort of Antalya. The dead included twelve British holidaymakers and in the days afterwards, Khalid Alfredi had again been determined as a key figure of interest.

Millî İstihbarat Teşkilatı, (MİT) the Turkish state intelligence agency apprehending a taxi driver responsible for transporting one of the bombers to the hotel had secured, under interrogation, information pinpointing several apartments and warehouses used in the planning and set up of the attack which Falcon had previously linked to Alfredi.

With the Egyptian already on the watch list as a known terrorist collaborator for his material aid and support to various right-wing and fundamentalist groups targeting western interests across Europe and the Middle East, the order had come down to find, fix and finish the man who was a key link in the chain between the financiers of the operations and their triggermen.

Shepard took a set of night vision goggles (NVGs) from Mills and placed them over his now back-to-front baseball cap, leaving the bracket popped up for the moment.

"Ops centre confirm the drone footage. There's nine heat signatures inside the compound. Two outside the west entrance, two kitchen, two lounge, and two in the suite with one in the room adjacent. No visual but based on the intel packet they're confident it's Alfredi," said Mills as Token and Gash, having sufficiently stowed the dirty laundry in the back of the van, dropped back to the paved drive.

"Gash, remain in overwatch and any changes get straight on the net with a heads-up and then away. Secondary RV as agreed," said Shepard. His orders were met with a grunt of acknowledgement from the trooper.

The parameters for the mission had been set days before with the team leaning on what they had learned early in their respective special forces careers, that the enemy was at its most vulnerable in the small hours before dawn when the human body's natural resistance was at its lowest ebb and in the place where they felt most comfortable, which in this case was a multi-million dollar resort complex surrounded by armed guards and the well-greased palms of a local police force.

Tonight, with no invitation, Shepard, Mills and Token would infiltrate Alfredi's retreat, eliminate any resistance, then seize the terrorist intermediary. With the target secure, Trident would return to the vehicle and they would exit together to their primary exfiltration point but if for any reason the hit should be compromised the three, plus their prisoner, would exit through an adjacent property to be collected on the shore two kilometres along the coast while Gash would dump the van and take secondary transport and retreat to the Turkish border.

Alfredi's days of financial support and collaboration were about to come to a sudden end, however, the grisly reality of his situation would come later and at the hands of others when his knowledge of the organisations he worked for, their hierarchies, finances and operations would be put under the uncomfortable glare of a spotlight somewhere far off the grid.

With Task Force Falcon's electronic surveillance, Shepard's days of reconnaissance and the arrival on station of the drone and its high-resolution IR (Infra-Red) imaging and real-time updates they were as prepared and as confident as they could be for a successful outcome.

Over his earpiece, Shepard listened to the calm voices from the tactical operations centre (TOC) who were directing the other pieces in the deadly game.

"Ready?" said Shepard.

The team, to a man, nodded their heads.

"Remember, there may be non-combatants inside, so check your shots."

"Roger, boss," said Token, verbalising the nodding heads of the other men.

Gash slapped Mills on the shoulder before stepping up into the cab of the van to monitor the operational communications traffic and that of corrupt elements of the local law enforcement whom they knew to be affiliated with, and acting as a quick reaction force for, the Egyptian lynchpin and other criminal elements in the town. Shepard gave a nod, and the troopers moved out.

Mills and Token, each equipped with identical Colt C8 CQB Carbine rifles, edged rapidly along the shrubbery and trees of the driveway towards the pool house where they then split to enter the rear patio from opposite sides, moving to secure the space with overlapping fields of fire.

Shepard dropped off the driveway via a set of marble steps and into a sunken garden, letting his eyes adjust to the shadows and saving the night vision device for when they breeched the interior. He moved quickly, the sights of his suppressed USP pistol up and covering his front arcs for any of Alfredi's men moving to investigate the sudden power cut. The element of surprise would last until they realised that the neighbouring villas were still lit up and their power supply hadn't tripped.

The path to the lower tier patio area was paved, aiding his silent approach. Moving carefully, Shepard skimmed tall ferns overhanging from beds of herbs and flowering plants, the scent of jasmine and mint heavy in the air as he weaved between sculpted topiary to rise up another few steps, pausing in the lee of a pergola, thick with flowering bougainvillea at the edge of the patio.

Muted voices floated on the humid night air, the tone giving no sign they had any awareness of the impending storm.

Shepard took a long slow breath, visualising the scene, the obstacles and the adversaries on the other side, feeling the familiar tremor of fear and anxiety that arose before focusing the emotions into a pinpoint beam of swift violence.

He knew which guard he would kill first, how the second would react, and then the exact route around the fallen men he would take to access the lower ground floor of Alfredi's villa.

His SELEX headset clicked, giving him the signal. Mills and Token were in position.

He acknowledged with a silent double click of

confirmation then stood and rolled around the corner of the pergola.

The first man rose from his plastic lawn chair and was stretching out the kinks in his back as Shepard stepped out of cover. The second guard extended his legs into the space cleared by his comrade and tipped his head back in a noisy yawn.

Both were oblivious as the SBS captain weaved between two twisted stemmed bay trees and swept the USP onto his first target, zeroing the sight and squeezing the trigger. The impact of the double rounds tipped the yawning guard over the back of his chair and onto the patio, then with a quick flick of the wrists, a second double volley sent the second guard's body from rigid surprise to fold limply in on itself.

Shepard silently crossed the now undefended space to the black-framed, bi-fold doors leading into the building. The rapid footfalls of Mills and Token were just audible as they fell in behind him.

Trident had rehearsed the next phase in a mock-up of the villa so many times it was ingrained into their muscle memory to the point they could have negotiated the inside space blindfolded. Shepard dropped his aim to the ground as Token depressed the door's handle, easing the frame aside to concertina in on itself and as soon as there was enough access the captain stepped inside, dropping the bracket of his NVGs to illuminate the darkened space beyond in hues of brilliant green.

Mills followed, peeling left with Token bringing up the rear and following on his heels, rifle up and sweeping arcs across the centre of a room dominated by a marble-topped island and breakfast bar. Shepard continued his rapid move to the right, clearing the garden diner to the spot where it opened through an archway into a lounge area. As he approached the threshold the dim sound of voices drifted from the other side.

"...I am just saying. That bomb will drop a target on our damn heads. It will be obvious those cretins had help in the execution."

The clunk of a glass being set down followed by a sigh preceded a tired response.

"Be quiet. Alfredi knows what he's doing," said a second unseen voice. The scent of cigarette smoke drifted on the draught from an open doorway.

"Does he? Getting directly involved in the killing of tourists is the wrong move." The first speaker sounded tense.

"The radicals will take the fall for the killings. There is no reason to think anyone is even aware of our involvement. Trust Alfredi," said the second man, aiming for reassurance in his pitch.

"I do. I just don't agree with us taking these kinds of risks."

"You'll take the money though?" The second speaker's tone fell to condescending and was followed by a chuckle.

Shepard eased closer to the edge of the archway and had a sliver of sightline to see two men facing away from him, leaning on a balcony railing and surveying the still night settling over the villa gardens.

He flinched as a voice cried out in surprise behind him. The two men spun around.

Mills reacted first as the man entered from the lounge. From his dress, he was a maintenance man or janitor. In one hand he held an electronic multimeter and in the other a screwdriver, but his effort to unearth the mystery power cut was suddenly forgotten.

The SBS trooper took three swift strides and slammed the stock of his rifle into the man's temple. The violence of the blow dropped him like a stone.

"Contact left." Token's voice was calm and clear over the net as the bulk of a new target framed the opening to the chef's kitchen, a gruff voice calling out in surprise and then charging at Mills.

Shepard swore to himself, knowing they had to move quickly now the element of surprise was unravelling. If they were caught up in a protracted fight, it could give Alfredi the opportunity to slip their grasp or to alert his local constabulary backup. He moved forward decisively.

Token snapped off two quick shots but the big man barrelled into his oppo nonetheless and the two men crashed over the island, scattering the cutlery and condiments sitting on top.

Shepard raised his USP and fired. His shots were accurate and caught his first target on the clavicle and then the cheek, knocking him sideways onto an armchair. Taking two strides forward into the lounge, his next volley caught the second rushing guard centre mass and as he crumpled to his knees, Shepard fired a third round into the top of the man's head.

Mills butted the face of the guard who now had a vicelike grip around the SBS trooper's throat. The burly guard grunted with effort as he pressed his advantage. Mills' legs scrambled for purchase until suddenly the grip loosed and his attacker arched backwards as though electrocuted, coughing up a lungful of bloody spittle. His big shovel-like hands flapped over his shoulders in a futile attempt to reach his back and as he twisted away and crashed against a double refrigerator, Mills spotted the blade plunged into his upper back.

Token stood beside the knife block and swept his C8 CQB to draw a bead on the writhing man now he was clear of his colleague but Mills got there first, drawing his own weapon from the countertop and stitching four rounds into the guard's chest.

Shepard entered and reached out a hand to aid Mills back to his feet.

Somewhere above, a raised voice sounded, followed by the clatter of something heavy hitting the floor.

"Six-two, six-one. Be advised weapons hot. Moving to first floor," said Shepard into his SELEX.

"Six-two received," acknowledged Gash from the gatehouse.

Shepard continued, reporting into the TOC as he led the way through the lounge to the hallway and its floating staircase that led to the first floor and Alfredi's suite.

"X-ray, Six-one. Tango's down. Moving to secure subject."

"Six-one confirmed. Be advised drone shows motorcade leaving provincial barracks and heading in your direction." The voice of the comms operator was steady, toneless and without concern.

Shepard bit back an oath at the news.

"Roger, X-ray."

The three troopers moved in single file out into the hallway and hugged the wall, first Shepard's and then the other trooper's weapons whipping up to cover the landing balustrade and stairway.

"Six-two, be advised company inbound. Prep for exit," said Shepard, receiving a double click of acknowledgement from Gash.

"Six-one, X-ray. Drone surveillance shows convoy is routing away from your position. Proceed with extraction."

"Six-one, roger." Shepard dropped the sights of his suppressed pistol over the space at the top of the stairs and slowly ascended; Mills and Token in line behind covered the arcs, left and right. Whatever had launched the locals, it wasn't their incursion, not yet at least.

Muted voices greeted them again as they graced the landing and turned left toward the double doors of the master suite. One voice, in particular, was louder than the others and sounded agitated and impatient.

The troopers' movements were silent, footfalls dampened by the thick pile of luxurious cream carpet as they approached the target.

Shepard felt the tension creep up his back as he moved within three metres of the door, sensing Mills move slightly to the right to offer more support and cover of the doorway ahead.

He was reaching out when the door was snatched open.

"Khalid…."

The woman in the bed sat up, scowling when she spotted Joumaa who remained standing by the suite's door with his usual dour expression.

"Khalid, what's going on. Where are you going?"

Alfredi ignored her as he shrugged an arm into a white shirt, glowering at his phone on the desk.

"Have you a signal?" he asked Joumaa.

The bodyguard pulled his phone free and looked at the screen, replying to the question with a stiff shake of his head.

"Shit," said Alfredi. He pulled the drawer of his desk open

and took out a Beretta 92X, racking the slide to ensure there was a round in the chamber, then he inserted a portable data drive into the MacBook and launched an app.

As he waited for the data to download, he picked up a short summer dress discarded on the floor and tossed it towards the bed. "Get dressed, Viktorija. We have to leave."

"But it's the middle of the night-"

Alfredi tore his MacBook from the docking station and looked again at the blank signal strength indicator on his iPhone, shaking his head in frustration.

"Shut up and get dressed," snarled Alfredi. "Have the police been in contact?" he asked of his head of security.

"No. We've had no indication anything untoward is occurring, but I've been on the roof and we are the only property without power," said Joumaa.

"So the question is, have higher authorities curtailed assistance from our friends?"

"You pay them to be loyal, Khalid."

"And they will be loyal until someone pays them more than me. Get some of the men up here and dismantle the rest of the hard drives and collect anything that may be of value to the authorities or our employers. I take it the yacht is ready?"

"The captain was told to be on standby for departure at short notice."

"Good." Alfredi tucked the MacBook under his arm and shot the two fingers of Don Julio 1942 tequila that remained in the glass on his desk. He blew out a breath as he clunked the receptacle back down.

It was highly unlikely his contacts within the local constabulary could have been gagged without him being tipped off to whatever operation was running against him, however, there were two very distinct and frankly frightening options that could explain the perilous situation.

Either the western governments had uncovered his links to the Turkey attack and brought their teeth to bear, persuading the local government it was in their interest not to harbour a known terrorist financier less they face political retribution and international sanctions or, his very careful manipulation of his employers' finances had been uncovered and they were about to show him thieves were not tolerated nor shown mercy.

He grabbed a pair of heels from the floor and thrust them into Viktorija's hands, hustling her barefoot towards the suite's door, hoping very much as Joumaa hauled it open, it was the former because the chances of surviving the latter were flat out zero.

Shepard snapped his weapon an inch to the right as a woman's face was backlit in the doorway. Behind her loomed a large brooding man who he recognised as one of Khalid Alfredi's close protection officers. The bodyguard's eyes betrayed surprise at suddenly facing armed soldiers, but his training and reactions kicked in to override the shock and save his life.

He shoved the woman into the firing line and kicked the door closed.

Shepard charged forward and squeezed the trigger at the rapidly narrowing entrance and as the woman toppled across his field of fire, he was rewarded by a mist of blood spraying the wall and the angry grunt confirming a hit on the man inside the room.

Mills stalled his own momentum and dragged the screeching woman from the floor and into the cover of a doorway as the boom of pistol shots splintered the suite's door.

Alfredi's wounded guard emptied his magazine, suppressing the raiders in an attempt to buy another few valuable seconds.

Shepard winced as the shattered shards of each strike exploded onto the landing, the splinters stinging his cheeks.

Across the hall, Mills had the woman pressed to the ground and was pulling a set of zip-ties from his belt to secure her.

As the initial salvo of gunfire ceased, Shepard shoved off the wall and when he was close enough, raised his heel and struck the door below the ornate handles, crashing the heavy mahogany inwards against the blood-smeared interior wall.

Moving through a mist of wood and plaster dust, he swept his gunsights across the room in search of a threat.

A crash from his left drew his aim, and he popped another two shots at the retreating figure of the bodyguard, the rounds studding the doorframe but missing his target.

"Contact left, left, left," he reported into the SELEX.

"Roger, left." Token hurdled an upended drinks trolley and gave chase, his rifle up and moving after the retreating guard, aware from reconnaissance photos and their mock-up training that the doorway he was exiting led to a lounge with its own internal spiral staircase into the garage space on the floor below.

"Six-one, troops in contact. One civilian secured. Moving to secure primary," said Shepard. The voice of the TOC operator calmly confirmed receipt of his update.

Weaving between contemporary armchairs and a low amber-topped coffee table, Shepard approached the master suite.

"Six-one, six-two. Prepare for exfil."

The SELEX warbled and blipped as Gash responded in acknowledgement.

"Roger that. Exit is clear. T-minus one-five mikes on the countdown."

Shepard mentally began to count down the remaining minutes until the anticipated return of Alfredi's police vanguard, momentarily considering his options if they appeared early. Whatever had spooked the column of police vehicles to leave their barracks, a confrontation with the locals would be an operational and political disaster and something to be avoided at all costs, regardless of any irregular allegiances they might have with his target.

The door to the master was ajar, and he paused at the threshold, taking cover against the edge of the door frame before gently pushing the door inwards, anticipating another salvo of shots which mercifully didn't come.

Rolling off the frame, he entered the suite, senses tuned for any sight, sound or motion that would give away the primary's location.

The room was large and open plan with very little in the way of cover or hiding place. The centre of the room was dominated by a wraparound sofa suite and with the bed arranged to offer a panoramic view of the sea.

Neither piece of furniture showed any tell-tale signs of recent use, nor did the wet bar in the corner seem to hold any bottles or glasses to suggest the villa's tenant had been caught in the throes of celebration or entertainment.

Moving around the perimeter to clear the master en suite and the walk-in closet, Shepard felt a momentary tremble stir beneath his feet before his irises constricted under the glare of an incoming flash. A heartbeat later, the floor to ceiling windows shuddered as a nearby explosion lit the room, the rumbling boom and shock wave rocking across the rooftops to slam the villa.

"What the hell..." Shepard strode to the en suite and kicked the door open, clearing the room and the shower stall.

"Six-one. X-ray. Report. Drone calls explosion approximately point five kilometres from your Alpha."

"Six-one, X-Ray. I see it..." Shepard paused as the tell-tale sound of automatic gunfire erupted down the street. "Heavy contact in progress at Bravo."

Quickly traversing the room from en suite to closet, he confirmed what his gut was now telling him.

"X-Ray, primary is not at this location. Repeat, we are negative on the target."

"Six-one, sit-rep acknowledged..." A hush fell over the comms as the TOC discussed the revelation. Seconds later, with a buzz and blip, their return to active communication sounded. "Six-one, X-Ray. Mission abort."

Shepard looked out the window at the muzzle flashes illuminating the gardens and treeline of the property further along the seafront and the firework display of tracer rounds cutting up the front of the villa. Periodic potshots from the building's out-gunned defenders flashed from low garden walls and windows.

His SELEX warbled.

"Six-two. Skip, time to go." There was an air of tension in Gash's voice and Shepard quickly worked out why as he followed the roadway northeast to where the flare of blue lights was descending quickly towards the scene and he felt a knot form in the pit of his gut.

Something wasn't right.

They'd had Khalid Alfredi in their sights, confirmed this was his retreat and now here they were inside, absent a primary target with a full-scale assault underway two streets across and the local blues and twos coming in hot.

Shepard looked around the room. It wasn't staged or sanitised, nor did it look abandoned at short notice. It was just a normal high-end suite awaiting its client.

Tugging open the desk and bedside cabinet drawers, he found them devoid of contents. Had they got it wrong or had someone tipped Alfredi the wink and he had quietly moved from his safe house? The operational command structure was tight so if there was a leak it had come from the inside, not unheard of, but given his trust in the people involved it was perhaps more likely that loose lips or poor operational practice by one of the support teams had revealed just enough to allow a whisper to get out and for Alfredi to join the dots.

A secondary explosion grabbed Shepard from his thoughts and the crackle of gunfire rippling down the street focused him on an immediate course of action. Whatever was happening nearby and, connected to Alfredi or not, his team couldn't be caught up in the crossfire or the aftermath.

As the blue lights and the wail of sirens drew closer, he felt an overwhelming nausea sweep over him, an unsubstantiated but feral fear that if he hung about much longer and his team were apprehended, they would become convenient scapegoats for a disgruntled partner government to hang the carnage upon.

He took one last look around the vacant suite before activating the SELEX.

"Six-one, Trident. All callsigns. Goliath, I say again goliath. Abort, abort, abort."

Chapter 1

Undisclosed CIA Facility, Vlaška, Romania. One month later.

Christmas Porter dropped a wad of gum into a waste receptacle and paused to let a ground crew manually manoeuvre the sleek airframe of an MQ-1 Predator drone across the tarmac and into the same hangar as she was heading to.

She took a moment to get her thoughts in order as she observed the crew, pulling her blonde hair up into a sleek ponytail and hooking her Ray-Ban aviators into the neck of a Converse tee shirt. The senior crew chief offered a nod of gratitude which she returned. The interior of the hangar was a hive of activity as maintenance teams worked on aircraft and vehicles and a group of soldiers in civilian casuals checked boxes of kit and weapons.

The facility had no official designation; it was funded off any official books and fell under the beyond-top secret purview of the Joint Special Operations Command comprising US, UK and allied Special Forces units and intelligence apparatus of which Christmas Porter was liaison and intelligence officer for the formidable Task Force Trident.

The air temperature inside the hangar was distinctly chillier than that on the sun-bleached tarmac, but Porter was grateful for the freshness as she followed the painted walkway leading towards the rear bunker section and her destination; the secure conference facility referred to as 'The Box'.

The intelligence officer was acutely aware that in just a few moments her briefing would crank the temperature of the already claustrophobic meeting space up to red-hot and ignite inter-agency rivalry to searing levels of cutthroat competitiveness. She smiled to herself. It was all in a day's work.

'The Box' resembled a large cargo container but the shabby effect masked hundreds of thousands of dollars of anti-surveillance and eavesdropping electronics which, combined with state-of-the-art materials, created a Faraday Cage, shielding the top-secret briefings and analysis within from any rival government agency who, if they did know of its existence, may have been trying to listen in.

There was only one heavy steel door set into its rust coloured sides and access was gained via a set of metal steps which were flanked by an armed and uniformed Marine sergeant.

"Ma'am."

"Sergeant." Porter nodded a greeting. The credentials she had slung around her neck were inconsequential to her securing entrance as her role and her reputation preceded her.

Badging her identification pass, she entered through an interlocking door into the facility proper.

A narrow lobby opened into what was a modest conference room. A lozenge-shaped table took up the bulk of the space with eight, wheeled office style chairs around the edge. The opposite wall from the entrance held a dozen clocks showing the time in various hotspots around the globe and to the head of the table, a short floor space allowed room for presentation onto one of the three small screens currently displaying satellite imagery or onto the larger electronic display that dominated the rear wall.

Two of the chairs were occupied while a third man, leaning on a work surface, slugged a mug of what she knew to be black coffee. An urn and a tree of white mugs were set on the surface to his right.

"Miss Porter."

"Colonel. Gentlemen," said Porter in greeting, first to the officer commanding the joint special forces command and Task Force Trident, Colonel Duncan McPeak, and then to her two intelligence contemporaries, David Yorke and Giles Hammond.

McPeak was greyhound thin and obsessively fit for a man of his rank and age. He wore military fatigues but, as was standard within the operations group, no rank insignia. Anyone assigned knew exactly who McPeak was.

Pushing fifty the colonel had been there and done it, having extensive experience of command at platoon and battalion level and eager to shun the rat race of further promotion to the general staff after post 9/11 campaigns in Iraq and Afghanistan and then during the Arab Spring he chose a different path.

McPeak had pursued the route into Trident as a means to sate his need for adrenaline and his desire to direct the tip of the spear against those enemies who still believed that striking from the shadows against the West and her allies offered a measure of security.

"I hope this is good, Porter because I've just spent fourteen hours trying to sleep upright and having my fillings shaken out inside an angry C-130." David Yorke slouched in his chair with a petulant pout. Like Porter, he was casually dressed. Blue denims with boating shoes and navy shirt under a loose and unzipped plain grey hoody. His compatriot from the United Kingdom Secret Intelligence Service (SIS), formerly known as MI6, was altogether more refined in his manner and welcome.

Giles Hammond looked like he had been delivered by luxury liner. He wore a wool blend jacket over a pristine Oxford shirt in a pale blue check which was tucked into navy formal trousers and his shoes had the sheen of parade ground polish.

"Pleasure to see you again, Miss Porter. I had the privilege of a British Airways upgrade so I may have an advantage over our colleague," said Hammond, rising to offer his hand.

Porter shook it, then moved to take a mug and slug in a bracing measure of the strong coffee.

"David's never happy. I'm over it," she said with a grin.

"That's not fair. I was ecstatic to hear from you. It was just that I thought you were calling to pay your debts from the Yemen op."

Porter rolled her eyes.

"I think we've been over this…"

"Yeah, your Special Activities boys fucked up, and I had to use my contact to bail you out…"

"We wouldn't have needed bailing out if your source hadn't played us and the courier in the first place. If anything, you owe Giles for losing him his financier."

Yorke made a face that crept into a grin and shrugged. "You win some, you lose some."

"Swings and roundabouts, as the saying goes," offered Hammond magnanimously.

Porter nodded and masked her true feelings with another swig of coffee. In truth, the loss had to smart.

The Yemeni Civil War had been raging for years and although violent and bloody, it had very little of the publicity of other headline conflicts and similar to what was befalling Syria, it had become a proxy for trans-national conflict. The frontlines shifted daily as Saudi Arabia and her allies aligned with the Yemeni cabinet and the national army pitted themselves against the Iranian, Iraqi and Syrian regimes and the swelling numbers of Islamic militant groups like Hezbollah, Al Qaeda and the Islamic State of Iraq and the Levant (ISIL) flooding into the country.

Hammond had been cultivating assets in the region for months in an attempt to sever a money trail that was financing murder on the streets of Europe. A swathe of terror attacks blighting capitals and media institutions over the previous year had been linked to a group operating inside Yemen who were engaged in training and equipping would-be jihadists for their holy war.

Managing a convoluted pipeline of sources, Hammond had eventually been led to a courier known as 'The Moth', his moniker derived from his fleeting nocturnal appearances.

The courier was a link between the militant factions and a shadowy group of wealthy Saudis and mystery investors who seemed to be playing both ends against the middle, making millions from the conflict by supplying weapons and munitions while undermining the coalition by targeting the public in shopping centres, hotels and beach attacks and making more money shorting positions on the currencies of those countries affected.

The mission to snatch the financier, and establish a route to the shadowy consortium pulling the strings, was put in play when one of Hammond's sources brought in a gentleman claiming to be 'The Moth's' landlord. The subsequent raid descended into chaos when the operators were ambushed, leaving two men dead and a third with life-changing injuries. 'The Moth' and his landlord didn't fare much better. Both were found hanging from telegraph poles within the week.

The route to the financier was cold, as was any chance of establishing a way to further expose the consortium funnelling their dirty war through him.

Porter set down her cup and approached the head of the table, collecting an iPad which lay on a shelf under one of the screens. She logged in with her secure identification codes.

"Well, the roundabout has come full circle," she said. The large screen behind her illuminated, directed into four smaller screens mirroring each of the open windows on the iPad. Porter looked to Colonel McPeak, and he nodded for her to proceed, taking a seat on the opposite side of the table to the two spooks.

"Task Force Cipher have been following a number of transactions that were exposed following seizure of IT equipment and documents in the Yemen raid." Porter highlighted a section of the screen showing emails, wireless transfers, and bills of lading.

"Electronic surveillance and covert intercepts have identified a match of transfers through banks in Sofia, Riga, and Gdansk. The funds are associated with accounts tied to the short-selling of stock in advance of recent terror attacks and with the shipping network of a large scale OCG operating out of Tunis. We have been unable to trace the transactions back to source however, both are linked to payment accounts we have identified as belonging to this man." Porter pulled the surveillance photo up front and centre.

"For crying out loud, Porter. You're bringing us a goddam ghost," said Yorke. He rolled his eyes and then leaned forward, resting on his elbows. McPeak raised a hand and waved the CIA officer's protest down.

"We've had ironclad intelligence on this character before, Miss Porter. How much more reliable is your information this time," said the colonel, his eyes narrowed as the cogs whirred in his mind at the sudden appearance of a familiar face.

"As reliable as it's going to get, sir. Khalid Alfredi has reached out to us through an intermediary. He wants to come in."

"Bullshit, Porter…"

"Mr Yorke," snapped McPeak in a display of the frustration which occasionally boiled over when interrupted or he was presented with overly complex or ill-thought ideas. "Hold your horses until the lady gets to the interesting part." He returned his eyes to Porter. "I was led by intel briefings to believe our friend Alfredi here had fallen off the map after Sozopol?"

"That's true. It seems that Alfredi's secondary safe house was attacked at the same time as Trident's operation. There have been no reported sightings since and we determined he had gone to ground or been captured by an unknown party."

"And your assessment now?" said McPeak.

"Let's just say that according to our intermediary, those who were paying Alfredi's wages are now seeking to terminate his contract."

A quiet fell over the room as the trio sat at the table considered what had been presented. Porter lined up the second half of her brief and braced for the backlash. Hammond broke the silence first.

"Is it your opinion based on what you have that Alfredi is my financier?"

"It's not just my opinion. He's confirmed it. He is offering information on those OCGs for whom he provided material support and he's willing to identify the source of the leak which scuppered the Yemen raid and offer up his knowledge of upcoming attacks and on his benefactors. He has email addresses, account numbers, shipping routes, storage facilities and safe houses. He's bringing it all to the table."

"Christ, this is the mother lode if it's legit." Yorke blew out a whistle and leaned back in his chair, linking his hands behind his head. His feet jiggled, burning off the excited energy.

Hammond looked more sceptical.

"One assumes he is asking for something in return?" he said.

"Immunity from prosecution, a new identity and secure transportation to a location of his choosing."

"No money?" said McPeak.

"That it seems is the reason for his spectacular fall from grace."

"The greedy bastard had his hand in the till?" said Yorke.

"And he wishes to keep what he found." Porter looked around the table.

"Who's the intermediary?" said McPeak, his eyes narrowing as he considered the satellite image of a coastline that Porter had launched onto the briefing screen.

"Dhimitar Dhusku."

"Not a goddam chance—"

"Dhusku has offered the use of his compound on the Bay of Rodon as neutral ground for the meet and ensures security for both sides during the negotiations."

"Dhimitar Dhusku is a loose cannon—" said Yorke, trying to interject as Porter continued speaking directly to McPeak.

"Dhusku has been instrumental in providing key information on GRU operations in Albania. Giles, what do you have to say?"

"It's true, he's a vital source in monitoring Russian influence in the region, especially since the annexation of Crimea and their blatant attempts at influencing political decision making across eastern Europe and the Balkans. We've been working with him via his role as one of the principal contractors on the Trans-Adriatic Pipeline and much of what we've been given has been actionable."

"Do you trust him?" said McPeak.

"Not as far as I could throw him, Colonel, but he is a likeable bugger." Hammond smiled and crossed his legs as Porter zoomed the satellite shot of Dhusku's Mediterranean compound.

"Dhusku wants a limited presence and specifically has requested your man present as guarantor that we aren't going to nod our heads, then drop Alfredi off at a black site. Is that something you'd be able to facilitate?"

"You know I will or you wouldn't have brought me here. Carlton Gatlin is the man. He's been courting Dhusku for the better part of a year. He's a solid field agent."

"Colonel, hear me out," said Yorke, rising to his feet to pace in agitation. "I'm not saying what is on the table isn't worth going out on a limb for, but Dhimitar Dhusku swings with the wind. Giles is right, we can't trust him. I'm shocked he even came to us with the offer and didn't hand Alfredi over to the other guys."

"Maybe Alfredi has made it worth his while," offered Hammond.

"Bullshit. Whoever is calling for Alfredi's head will just as soon lop off the legs of anyone known to have harboured and assisted him."

"It's a chance worth taking," said Porter. McPeak narrowed his eyes and considered the risk versus the reward.

"What's the window," said McPeak.

"Two days. Dhusku will provide transport for Alfredi from his safe house and we negotiate the trade at the compound and then orchestrate his safe exit."

"Can your operative be in position inside that time, Mr Hammond?" said McPeak.

"Absolutely, Colonel."

"Do you have a negotiator in mind?" said McPeak. Porter nodded.

"Karen Miller. She looks like a lamb but is fierce as a lion."

"Security?"

Porter shook her head. "Dhusku wants it low key, so there won't be a full close protection unit. I do have someone in mind though. Just in case."

McPeak nodded.

"Draw up an initial plan. We'll review it in two hours."

Chapter 2

As Tom Shepard stepped into Hangar A, he was greeted with the gravelly commands of a gruff Delta Force sergeant who was breaking the hearts of the junior ranks under his command.

The big Yank had the expression of a bulldog chewing a wasp and barked encouragement and insults in equal measure as he hustled his crew to shift crates of munitions and equipment off the back of a low-loader and into a caged storage area set apart from the rest of the open floor.

He paused momentarily in his tirade to size up the newcomer who had invaded his kingdom but then lifted his chin in a greeting, recognising in the quiet confidence of the SBS captain the traits of a fellow apex predator.

Shepard winced inwardly as a young trooper lost grip of a crate and the wooden box smashed into the pockmarked concrete. The sergeant was in his face in a heartbeat, eyes bulging and his jaws chewing the younger man a new backside.

The last few hours had been a whirlwind following a few weeks of relative inaction since the Black Sea operation.

Having relocated back to the staging centre in Paderborn,

Trident's time had been spent undertaking after-action briefings on what had happened at the villa and the analysis of several phones and a laptop that had been recovered, none of which had yet to offer any leads other than Alfredi's supplier of high-class escorts, a penchant for pornography and his favourite takeaway restaurant.

The post mortem on the surprise attack on the property close by had also yielded very little in the way of actionable intelligence and any other information that was available publicly was being suppressed by local police and government officials who were putting the event down to infighting between criminal elements. In subsequent days, several local news outlets were running the story alongside a few grainy mobile phone clips shot from a distance alongside editorials condemning the influx of western criminals and cartels to the resort town. That angle was too much of a coincidence for Shepard and the spooks to swallow and the captain was confident something would shake loose, eventually.

When not in briefings or squaring away the assault kits, the team did what they did best, honing the razor's edge to ensure they were operationally ready no matter when the next call came or where it would send them.

Mornings were spent in the gym and on perimeter runs around the camp, strength and endurance workouts taking the edge off boredom and inaction while the afternoons were spent on the range keeping weapons zeroed and their sights and skills focused with weapon handling.

Evenings then passed around an outside grill, the big charcoal barbecue crippled with the weight of tenderloin and T-bone. Afterwards, with full bellies they rested on the battered old sofas in the mess, a tirade of quotes and impressions drowning out the soundtrack of the eighties action movies and sports re-runs, of which Gash's favourite was the one of Token's sister making her bid for the British Olympic Team; the banter of the latest re-run had been interrupted by a young lance corporal informing Shepard their commanding officer, Major John Canning required his immediate presence.

That had been seven hours and about two thousand kilometres ago.

Shepard offered little more than a nod or a courteous hello to the troops and support staff he passed on his way through the hangar, his stride measured him as a man on a mission although the calm exterior masked a mind swirling with thoughts of what the major had briefed him on and how it might relate to the failed raid.

The failure to seize the Egyptian had irked him and the feeling that the mission had been compromised from the off had never really left, the suspicion creeping around in the back of his mind as he drifted off to sleep or in the quiet minutes of the early morning. On the one hand, it was a blessing no one had been killed or captured, but on the other, he couldn't shake the notion their failure was predestined. That it had been someone's plan all along.

Whether the woman he was about to meet could shed any light on it remained to be seen but, fractious as their relationship could be at times and overlooking any irritation at being red-eyed to a remote CIA black site in the arse end of Romania he was looking forward to seeing Christmas Porter again.

* * *

"Apologies for the cloak and dagger, Captain. You're not too bleary, I hope."

"Not at all. The suspense is killing me though," said Shepard.

Christmas Porter nudged her glasses to a more comfortable position and gave him a tight smile. The case officer and the captain had, at times, endured a difficult working relationship, he being curtailed by convention whilst she operated in the grey realm between international treaties where rules were made to be broken or laws re-written to suit outcomes, nevertheless, they worked well together and since the Syrian mission to recover Porter's asset a scab of mutual professional respect had formed over any minor disagreements in how the other performed their job.

"Captain Shepard, it's good to see you."

"You too, sir." Shepard approached the conference table and shook the hand of the seated Colonel McPeak, taking the offered chair indicated. Porter remained standing, and Shepard offered a nod of acknowledgement to the five others stationed around the oval table.

A couple of them were new faces, another two he knew of but had no prior professional dealings, and the last he counted as a friend.

"Chad, she's roped you in too then?" said Shepard, a grin breaking his bearded face, mirroring the infectious smile of the Navy SEAL.

"I heard you were on board and couldn't say no." Chad Powell was six-two and sixteen stone of mayhem. The former college linebacker had enlisted shortly after 9/11 and eventually served alongside Shepard in Iraq and Afghanistan as part of the Joint Special Operations Group and Trident's predecessor, Task Force One-Twenty-One, the SEAL proving himself to be an adept warfighter. He was a man of quiet strength with a sharp intellect and a generous teammate. A bit of the tension eased from Shepard's spine in seeing him there.

"Introductions then," said Porter, taking a step forward, eager to get business underway.

"Captain Tom Shepard, Chief Petty Officer Chad Powell." Both men raised a palm in greeting to the eyes looking at them. "Gents, this is David Yorke, CIA and Giles Hammond, SIS."

Porter directed a hand at the two men who no longer sat beside each other but instead beside a respective counterpart. "Carlton Gatlin also SIS, and you both know Karen Millar," she finished indicating the small red-headed negotiator.

Shepard had seen the woman in action over a number of deployments with Trident, watching mesmerised as the seven stone soaking wet ultra-marathon runner went toe to toe against the heavyweights of the Pakistani ISI over access to Al Qaeda detainees and at her almost mystical ability to ingratiate herself to tribal elders and local militia commanders to gain intel on the suspects they hunted. Impressive for anyone outside their circle, but doubly so considering the group's deeply ingrained misogynistic values and male-dominated culture. Millar returned his nod with a smile.

"Apologies for the speed of calling you together and the secrecy. Unfortunately, time is of the essence on this one," said Porter. She looked at each of the newcomers, took a breath and launched her brief onto the large briefing monitor.

"You should all recognise this man. Khalid Alfredi. He is the primary target of this mission."

Shepard raised an eyebrow but Porter, although she looked him square in the face, made no acknowledgement. Whatever he had been expecting, it wasn't this. Not so soon after the last failure.

"It was my understanding Alfredi was in the wind," he said into the pause.

"He was, and now he's very much back on the table." Porter gave a trademark nonchalant shrug. "Don't look a gift horse in the mouth."

"That didn't work out so well for the Greeks, Christmas," said Shepard. McPeak gave a short snort.

"I understand your concern after last time, Captain. Miss Porter, we were confident of Alfredi's location and it bombed. Captain Shepard's team could have very easily been caught up in that shitshow that played out down the street. How confident are we this time?"

"But they didn't," said Porter with an easy smile, directing her focus on Shepard. "We're very confident, sir, and as a bonus, Tom now gets to redeem himself."

Shepard shook his head and bit back a smile at the case officer's needling. She addressed the newcomers when she spoke next, drawing up a further selection of images showing Alfredi on a yacht, exiting a supercar outside the Casino de Monte-Carlo and shirtless on a sun terrace looming over a much younger brunette.

"Alfredi wants to come in," she said. "For the benefit of those not quite so acquainted as Captain Shepard, Khalid Alfredi has been a priority target for Trident for some time." She drew a finger across the iPad to draw up a damning biography. "Khalid grew up in the slums of Cairo, aligning himself with the Muslim Brotherhood in the wake of the Mubarak overthrow. He was rounded up in the 2013 purges but managed to escape and exiled himself with some other mid rankers to Tunisia. It is unclear but in the intervening years Alfredi set up a funnel to facilitate smuggling and trafficking between North Africa and Europe." The current image on the screen showed a long-range reconnaissance photo of the Egyptian meeting a smaller, white westerner. The man's skin was lobster red in the blistering sunshine.

"This, for instance, is Ciaran Knox. He's wanted by the British and Irish governments over drug importation and for ten killings contributing to a feud between rival Irish gangs. We know Alfredi facilitates Knox's shipments and that he has put him in contact with several other big European distributors. Alfredi seems to be the lynchpin for a wider network of criminal facilitators and organised criminal gangs."

The image changed, but the context was familiar and each showed a healthy-looking Alfredi meeting more nefarious looking partners.

"As his influence grew, he began offering material aid and support for Islamist and far-right groups with axes to grind. Smuggling aside, his business now extends to weapon procurement, safe houses, transportation, and it seems his client base has grown to include a number who are pursuing direct action against our joint foreign policies, Hezbollah, Al Qaeda, ISIL and of more concern recently operations against our partners in Syria and Yemen. We can now tie him as the middle man in financing and support of at least two dozen attacks across Europe and our Middle Eastern area of operations and the recent suicide attack in Antalya."

"What's driving him into our arms now?" said Millar.

"It would seem he's been burning bridges." Porter clicked up some of the footage from the Sozopol safe house raid that had played out on local news sites, a garbled voice commentating over shaky phone footage of explosions, tracer and the rattle of gunfire.

"A month ago we launched an operation to seize Alfredi. The mission washed out, however, NSA and GCHQ have solid intercepts since that a price has been put on his head. To answer your question, Karen, it's self-preservation. He's been caught with his hand in the till."

"He doesn't strike me as a character of many redeeming qualities. Why are we helping his arse out of the fire?" said Gatlin.

"Quite simply, because he has ten years of intelligence rattling around inside his skull. Names, addresses, access to active terrorist and criminal cells and their bank accounts, details on historic atrocities and those in the pre-planning phase. He's going to give it all up to pay for his survival."

Shepard considered the sudden change of tack and wondered did this make things any easier. He wasn't sure it did, nor was the extremely limited number of players around the table filling him with confidence.

"Why is this briefing not to a full strike team?" he said.

Porter flicked the iPad and again the screen changed to show a satellite image of a coastal compound and a bearded gentleman in his mid-fifties. He was well dressed with a hint of the soft edges a life of luxury could impose on someone who had been hewn a little harder in youth.

"This is Dhimitar Dhusku," said Porter. "He is a principal

contractor on several large scale energy projects, but more importantly, he is an SIS asset and has reached out as Alfredi's intermediary." She turned to Hammond and gestured with an open palm. "Giles, would you like to give your input and how you and Carlton fit into this?"

The Englishman sat up a little straighter in his seat, resting the heels of his hands on the edge of the desk and steepling his fingers.

"Christmas has brought us in because Dhusku is one of our assets. He's a poacher turned gamekeeper of sorts, formerly serving in the Romanian Department of State Security until the fall of Ceausescu in eighty-nine. He made a mint during the collapse of the Soviet Union and maintains close contacts from his DSS days across industry and finance and with the Russian FSB." Hammond leaned back in his chair and glanced briefly at David Yorke.

"My counterpart across the table is less thrilled with Dhusku's involvement as he is known to skirt the lines of legality. The infiltration of organised crime across all sectors has seen corruption run rife and Dhusku's coffers have been swelling significantly given his monopoly control over labour, transportation and manufacture which is all down to the manipulation, threat and corruption of market forces by those he keeps his hands in with. It is our assessment this is how he came into contact with Khalid Alfredi and why we chose to court him."

"Dhimitar Dhusku is just another ex-Stalinist baton-wielder who's got rich and has aspirations to throw his hat in the political ring," said Yorke to Shepard. "Giles is looking to the future and would like to have someone like that on the payroll, but deep down Dhusku is a crook and I don't believe we should be placing our faith in him." He gave a general shrug and then a more pointed cock of the head at Colonel McPeak.

"It's a fair enough observation, narrowly looking at his history and his contacts, but given the Kremlin's current aggressive foreign policy and their surreptitious operations across Europe against some of our partners, he's an asset in the region. Carlton?"

Carlton Gatlin was caught in the middle of a sip of water. Swallowing quickly he deposited the glass and smoothed his plain navy tie.

"Dhimitar vividly recalls the austerity and the upheaval of revolution. He's been enjoying the benefits of growing economic ties to the west and the scaling of propaganda from Moscow and their active measures to destabilise the region have tipped him even closer to us. Change in London and Washington has helped, but ultimately he's embraced capitalism."

"If he's so keen to grab the dollar, how come he isn't handing Alfredi over to whoever wants him?" said Powell. Shepard nodded his agreement.

"Someone ratted him out at Sozopol. Chad's right, what's to say this isn't another lure?"

Christmas Porter cleared her throat, sensing Yorke was about to plunge in with both feet.

"Dhusku's involvement with Alfredi is obviously one of mutual benefit. It's my guess when Alfredi disappears with his airplane full of stolen loot, Dhusku will try to take advantage of the vacuum."

"You mean take over his clientele?"

"Not exactly. With the information Alfredi's delivering,

we're looking at the most comprehensive strike on organised crime and terror groups in several years. We could be talking a route into high-level terrorist planning and organisational structure. The roots will be dug up for years to come, but that leaves a void for Dhusku to exploit, perhaps some of which Alfredi has promised him for his support."

"I still don't like it," said Shepard.

"The captain is a good judge of character," said Yorke, giving the SBS operator a firm nod of support.

"The gains it would seem outweigh the risks." Hammond shrugged, his palms settling on the table.

"None of us like it, Tom, but it is what it is," said Porter. "In less than forty-eight hours at Dhusku's compound, Karen is going to negotiate Alfredi's surrender and his exit from the country. Carlton as Dhusku's case officer has been asked to vouch for the integrity of our offer and add his assurance that any deal struck is honoured."

"I assume once the deal's done, it's us moving Alfredi to a secure location. That's not giving us long to get the resources prepped and consider any constraints and contingencies?" said Powell.

Shepard caught the quick twist of Porter's lips and then the slight void of silence. McPeak broke the building tension.

"This won't be a team action. Carry on, Miss Porter."

"Colonel." She faced Shepard, her face set in an impassive mask. "Dhusku has offered to oversee the security of the meet and ensure the safety of both parties—"

"That's generous of him." Shepard butted in. The nagging feeling he'd had in Sozopol beginning to gnaw at him again.

"We have drone cover over the compound and on all inland routes, so should Alfredi choose a sea exfiltration or go by land, we have you covered."

"By that, you mean me and Chad?"

"Yes, I want you to be close protection during the meet and for the transfer. Don't let Alfredi out of your sight. Chad, you'll liaise with and support Dhusku's men in overwatch and then oversee the convoy's route out."

Shepard locked eyes with the big SEAL and could see he shared his anxiety over the strategic gaps. McPeak read the uncomfortable undercurrent and spoke.

"We'll have a ship-based quick reaction force on standby in the Adriatic. The caveat being they will be far enough away to give comfort to Mister Alfredi and not to offend Dhimitar Dhusku's offer of hospitality. They'll be close, but should anything go sideways you'll have to find a corner and dig in, understood?"

Shepard nodded his ascent, as did Powell. Neither man was in the business of shooting down the chain of command. McPeak looked around the table at the others.

"Good, now that the gents are up to speed, let's get down to brass tacks and understand what exactly we expect to be getting from this goddam merchant of death in exchange for getting him off his hook."

Chapter 3

Makarska, Adriatic Coast

Dieter Kline stubbed out his cigarette and wafted away the rising smoke. The scowl on his face was not due to the dying acrid tendrils stinging his eyes but the escalating rhetoric between the other two men on the call.

"You ensured us the last time this was in hand and the snake escaped." The Englishman's tone was clipped and hid little of his irritation that the matter in hand went unresolved.

"If you hadn't sent incompetent idiots the last time, we wouldn't need to be having this conversation."

"You said he was lightly defended," protested the Englishman.

"He was—"

"Enough," said Kline with a tone of finality cutting over the second speaker whose attitude had been aggressive and condemnatory from the outset.

The Bavarian mercenary easily intimidated most men, with a stature that seemed hewn from the peaks of the Alps and ice-blue eyes that were devoid of empathy. His mere presence undermined the confidence of the most unflappable opponent, but for whatever reason, be it arrogance or stupidity or the safety of being on the other end of the line the caller continued his diatribe despite the warning to cease.

"You need to remember your place, Dieter. We point and you shoot, you're not on this call to give orders—"

"And you need to remember that, at some point in the future, you and I are going to be in a room together. A telephone line will not protect you then." The German let the threat settle and for the first time during the protracted call the man shut up.

After several seconds, his English sparring partner picked up the conversation, trying to steer it back towards their common purpose.

"The consortium does not stand for insubordination," he said matter-of-factly. "Khalid has been an asset to us and it is regrettable we find ourselves on this path, but thieves must be made an example of. I think you can understand and agree on that?"

The caller continued to express his belligerence with a scoffing grunt of agreement.

Dieter rolled his eyes. The mercenary had little time for the man on the other end of the call, and although he had served his purpose in unearthing the whereabouts of the Egyptian thief, Kline passionately hoped that after that particular issue was dealt with, the consortium would issue the instruction to bury the source of the leak that had led them to the financier.

His faceless employers were ruthless. Their reach stretched like an invisible web across borders and jurisdictions, and their influence cut to the heart of political ideology and pulled at the strings of government through the insidious corruption of sovereign state legislature, executive and judiciary. Operating in the shadows, the secretive cabal of men and women bolstered their coffers through assiduous manipulation of geopolitical conflict and by exacerbating historic tensions between the big players, those activities enabling them to accrue vast quantities of illicit wealth which in turn purchased even greater global domination.

It wasn't Khalid Alfredi's theft nor that he could deliver names, accounts or partners that had signed the man's death warrant. He had broken trust and whilst he had escaped the noose once, this time he and those intent on harbouring him would be dealt with swiftly and violently, serving as an example that no one was out of reach no matter where they chose to hide.

"Of course I agree. For one it's my head in the damn vice. If Alfredi decides to implicate me in the murder of The Moth or any one of a dozen other operations, I'll be the one with a one-way ticket to a third world shit hole to have electrodes strapped to my balls and dirty water forced down my throat so stop questioning my motivation."

"It's not your motivation, it's your attitude," said Dieter. "Fear is affecting your decisions. Gather some focus and I will take care of Alfredi. When he's dead, you will have nothing to fear and you can continue your work."

"Fine, but understand this is out of my control now."

Dieter Kline resisted the urge to snap at the man's attempts to pre-emptively distance himself from failure.

"The consortium understands your position," said the Englishman, his tone more conciliatory than condescending. "Your work in bringing us this is appreciated."

The hum of static sounded into the silence before the Englishman continued.

"Can you be more specific about the information Alfredi intends to use to buy his freedom?"

"I can't. I'm informed it is of high value and the assessment is that it will have a significant impact on our efforts in the short to medium term but specifics or indeed any hard intel will only be handed over following negotiations."

"All the more reason to ensure we must be confident your time frame and target information are accurate."

"It's one hundred per cent accurate. The operation is in phase one and assets are en route to the staging area."

"Good, in that case, let us prepare to eliminate the cause of our concerns. On that, Dieter, can you handle the time frame?"

Kline nodded as he spoke, even though neither man could see him.

"I have had assets ready to move since Sozopol. We can be on the ground in six hours. I know Dhimitar Dhusku and am familiar with his bayside complex. It's a fortunate turn of events and offers an excellent opportunity to bring an end to this."

"Excellent," said the Englishman. "I think we need to send an unequivocal message. Everyone in that compound is to be eliminated, understood?"

"It will be done," said Kline.

"Well then, the clock is ticking. I expect updates as our former colleague arrives and on the status of the security present, there is to be no repeat of last time." The Englishman's tone left little wiggle room for his embedded colleague.

"I'll try. Once the operation is live, it will be hard to leave the situation room."

"Understood, but update as you can through the secure channel. Dieter, confirm when you get into position and wait for instruction to engage."

Kline didn't reply, tapping another cigarette out of the pack before placing it between his lips and flicking open his lighter. Taking a long, satisfying drag, he began to mentally check off his resources and run the raid through in his mind's eye. Detail was everything and this time Alfredi would not escape.

Chapter 4

Tirana County, Albania

"Jeez. It's like a frigging rollercoaster."

Karen Millar grabbed at the handhold above the rear passenger door as the driver of the lumbering Toyota 4Runner gunned the SUV across an intersection and onto another patch of questionably tarmacked road.

Shepard for the third time in as many minutes tried to ignore the guy's white-knuckled grip on the steering wheel and craned his neck to peer out of the windscreen at the lead vehicle setting the crazy cross country pace, scanning the arid landscape nudging up to the roadside for potential threats or unexpected diversions ahead.

At the moment, the only danger seemed to be the risk of them losing control on the loose gravel or a collision between the vehicles of the nose to tail convoy. Glancing down into the passenger wing mirror he eyed the vehicles behind. Each of the SUVs weaved in their wake as though on rails but the drivers' and passengers' faces within were obscured by the billowing dust his own vehicle was kicking up.

They were an hour into their journey from Tirana towards

the meet and neither the speed nor the erratic driving had abated from the second they had slammed the doors closed and bulldozed through the busy airport traffic. Once the CIA chartered G-5 jet had landed and taxied to one of the secluded private hangars at the edge of the airfield, they had been met by a representative of Dhimitar Dhusku, the SIS officer, Carlton Gatlin, leading the way and directing the small team into each of the four vehicles. Gatlin had taken the lead car with Dhusku's greeter, Shepard and Karen Millar were in the second car with Chad Powell following them. The tail of the convoy held a four-man team of Dhusku's security. Shepard had exchanged wary nods with the group at the hangar, but had no time to interact before Gatlin had jostled everyone into the cars. They had looked the business though, sharp eyed and muscular with a quiet confidence in how they held themselves, each wore a shoulder rig with holstered pistol and Shepard held little doubt that if required they would know how to handle themselves.

"Should we have brought you a sick bag off the plane?" said Shepard, shooting a glance and a grin over his shoulder at the lithe negotiator.

"I've a stronger stomach than you, Shepard, and you know it."

He gave a short chuckle and turned back to observe the road ahead.

"One of the last close protections I was on was Tripoli. The drivers were that bad a few of our lads took to taking motion sickness pills and wearing gum shields. No offence." He cocked an eyebrow at the driver, who maintained his focus straight ahead, seemingly oblivious to the conversation.

"Bullshit."

"I'm serious. These guys could ride a RIB in a force ten under fire, too," said Shepard. Millar laughed, the sound deadened by the thrum of rubber on tarmac and the whistle of the slipstream.

"How are you feeling?" she said.

Shepard glanced back again. Her green eyes sparkled with curiosity and intellect but the slight pinch between her eyebrows marked a degree of anxiety.

"Under-armed, undermanned, underprepared. Just a normal day at the office. You?"

Millar gazed out the window, her head lolling from side to side with the motion of the vehicle.

"Tense."

"It'll be fine, Karen. This guy wants to come in." He half turned in his seat, unrestricted by the seatbelt which was strung out and clipped in behind him. Millar's was pulled tight across her chest and she continued to grip the grab handle.

"The SIS spooks are hand in glove with this Dhusku fella and from what I can tell his guys seem clued in."

"Guys like Alfredi don't flip, Shepard."

"Most guys like Alfredi don't mug off their employers. These people don't take any prisoners."

"I know, I'm just nervous."

"When this kicks off, you're in charge. Just say the word and I'll pull us out." He gave a reassuring nod, which she returned. "Chad will be covering the exterior and I'll be right there. If I sense something, I'll give you notice and you can make the call."

Millar nodded. Shepard couldn't blame her for being tense. Something was nipping at him too. He prided himself on being a good traveller, you had to be when ninety per cent of insertions were by submarine, fast boat or helicopter, and he wasn't a control freak, normally content in putting his life in the hands of those professionals who had been tasked with delivering him into danger, but this time the SUV swaying on its suspension highlighted how much they were reliant on men they didn't know to get them to a location they hadn't had time to scout and chosen by a man with a dubious background. He looked across again at the driver, the white-knuckled joyride emphasising perfectly how much control had been taken out of his hands.

A sudden deceleration snapped his head back to the windscreen. The brake lights of the vehicle ahead burned, and the 4Runner eased right off the road onto a gravel shoulder. As it rolled to a stop, Shepard felt a tug in his gut. Blocking the exit were two Toyota Land Cruisers. Outside the vehicles, garbed in civilian clothing but toting ASh-82 assault rifles stood a half-dozen men of fighting age, one of whom walked forward and waved in the convoy, his voice barking orders.

"What's this? Who are these guys?" said Shepard, his hand slipping to the paddle holster on his hip and easing the H&K USP 9mm out and onto his lap.

"Do you understand me?" he nudged the driver, jerking his head towards the man now waving them in. "Amigo? Friendly?"

The driver shrugged. In the back seat, Shepard heard Millar unholster and cock her own sidearm. The 4Runner drew to a shuddering stop and the driver ratcheted the handbrake.

Before the gunman could close further, Shepard threw his

door open and stepped out. In almost the same instant, Carlton Gatlin in the lead vehicle did the same. The crunch of gears and scuff of tires from behind him gave Shepard notice that Chad Powell and the last vehicle in the convoy had also drawn in.

"Gatlin?" shouted Shepard above the noise of the idling engines, the USP in hand, but pressed tight against his thigh.

The gunman raised his assault rifle, aiming at Shepard. The stock collapsed and the barrel wavering along his midline. "No. No, poshte." He jabbed the weapon in Shepard's direction, voice thick with tension and his finger dropping from the guard onto the trigger. "Poshte!"

"For God's sake. He's telling you to put the weapon down," shouted Gatlin.

"Tell him to get that gun out of my face first."

Gatlin spoke a rapid burst, the translation lost to Shepard and doing little to calm the man or quell the escalating tensions. Shepard heard the door behind him open and Millar step out.

"Get back in the bloody vehicles," said Gatlin.

"What's going on, Carlton?" said Millar, walking past Shepard to put herself between the SBS captain and the gunman. She raised both palms and offered a gentle gesture of suppliance. Her own weapon was re-holstered at the small of her back.

"We are changing drivers," said Gatlin.

Dhusku's man who had met them at the airport stepped away from his discussion with the men and jerked his head back at the transport. "Please, do as Carlton says. It is for your own safety."

Shepard wasn't sure, and neither was the gunman by the

look in his eyes.

"We wish to maintain operational security for your meeting. These drivers will take us to the rendezvous," he said, waving back towards the men gathered around the Land Cruisers. There was more chance of finding horns on a shark than this new contingent being replacement drivers, thought Shepard.

"The meet is at Dhusku's villa. The world and his wife knows exactly where that is so changing drivers isn't going to maintain shit," said Shepard.

"The location has changed."

Shepard heard Chad Powell swear and hawk a gob of spittle on the roadside.

"Changed when?" said Shepard.

"That's of no concern."

"Gatlin, explain to your friend here we'll walk and leave his boss and Alfredi to take their chances if he doesn't start playing ball." Shepard pointed at the SIS man's contact. To his left, the gunman remained in a defiant pose.

"I have authority here and I can vouch for these men," said Gatlin, frustration creeping into his voice. He dabbed his forehead with a handkerchief. "Just do as they say and get back in the cars, we're exposed out here."

Shepard took a glimpse up and down the road. In the few minutes they had been parked, no traffic had passed by, and as he thought about it, there hadn't been much on the roads at all since they left the outskirts of the last town. He supposed there could be an outer cordon funnelling traffic away and ensuring the speed of the transfer but an unexpected hard stop and change of location made him anxious.

"You need to call it in," said Millar, coming to the same conclusion Shepard was reaching. If they needed the QRF, someone had to know where to send it.

"I'm not calling it in. Any communication could be compromised." Gatlin shook his head, then shrugged "We'll notify safe arrival, will that do?"

The gunman seemed to sense the conflict and jerked his rifle towards the 4Runner.

Shepard, low on options and not in a position to override the SIS officer chose to avoid the potential for an accidental discharge and turned back to the Toyota, holding open the door for Millar. As he thumped it closed, he gave Chad Powell a look, the communication non-verbal but crystal clear: get your head on a swivel and your wits about you. Improvise, adapt, overcome.

Powell responded with a quick dip of his head and Shepard got back in the 4Runner, a headache creeping up the back of his skull and his nerves jangling.

Chapter 5

Krujë District, north-central Albania

The convoy rolled to a stop and their new driver bid Shepard remain seated and then he got out, taking the keys with him.

"What the hell is Gatlin playing at?" said Shepard, twisting in his seat to get a view around the 4Runner and not liking what he saw.

They were the second vehicle in the line and all of them were boxed in bumper to bumper, kerbside in a busy street that opened into an even busier market square. To the immediate passenger side was a line of shops with windows and wares shaded by coloured awnings and at his eleven o'clock the tired facade of what may once have been an opulent hotel.

People swarmed all around them as they weaved along the pavement. The sound of voices, the toot of horns and the rev of engines joined in the raucous cacophony.

Behind him, Millar shifted restlessly.

"We were supposed to be doing this off the radar in Dhusku's compound." Millar's head swivelled left to right, watching pedestrians skirt them on the pavement, an occasional bemused face peering in as they carried provisions away or ambled lazily towards the covered market on the other side of the wide plaza. She flinched as a motorbike screeched to a stop beside her window. A heartbeat later, it weaved into the ribbon of traffic.

"I don't like this."

"You're telling me," agreed Shepard, trying to get his bearings.

After the stop, they had turned north and continued along the coast, travelling another three-quarters of an hour until they hit the outskirts of civilisation. It had taken about five more minutes to reach their current destination. From his initial briefing and study of the geography in and around Dhusku's compound, he put them at a small town about thirty kilometres inland.

As he continued his track of the faces in the crowd for anyone that looked glaringly out of place, he noticed the doors of the hotel open and two burly men in sunglasses exit onto the pavement. In the vehicle ahead, the two front doors opened and Gatlin and Dhusku's greeter exited to the pavement.

"Looks like game on. Stay here a minute…"

"He said to wait in the—"

Shepard was already out and Millar's protest was muffled as he closed the door.

The two heads outside the old hotel turned and he noted a hurried exchange of conversation with the approaching Gatlin. Both men's demeanour stiffened as Shepard walked towards them and he self-consciously let his hands hang by his sides, palms open and facing forward.

The chatter of patrons in the cafes and between

shopkeepers and customers buzzed in his ears, no one seemingly paying any attention to the sudden arrival of a group of SUVs. Away to his far right and walking towards the plaza, a mixed group of flag-waving and chanting men and women drew the ire of the traffic, the toots increasing as what looked like a protest spilled onto the roads.

Shepard's attention was drawn back ahead as the nearest man outside the hotel took a step forward to intercept his path. Although matched in height, the man outweighed him by at least fifty kilos. His big gut protruded over the top of beige slacks and his nylon polo shirt strained around his neck, the material losing the fight against the flab and the tufts of thick body hair sprouting up from his back.

Shepard realised the palm's open gesture of submission wasn't going to do the trick, probably because as his body language presented compliance; his face screamed mutiny.

"Problem?" he said as he neared the Englishman.

"No problem," said the greeter with an easy smile on his face, waving off the gorilla and turning to face the taller SBS captain.

"Gatlin?" Shepard reiterated.

"No problem here. Give me one moment to confirm a few details and then we can get inside."

"What's with the relocate?" Shepard addressed the query as much to Dhusku's man as Gatlin.

The spook gave a small shake of the head and a smile of the type reserved for impatient children.

"It's perfectly safe—"

"This isn't a good idea."

"As I said—"

"Have you called in the divert?" said Shepard, Gatlin's

expression giving him the answer he didn't want.

"My friends here represent the local constabulary," said the greeter to whom Shepard had yet to be formally introduced. "They have carried out a dry clean of the premises and are running active surveillance on all routes in and out of the square. Dhimitar Dhusku extends you his hospitality and his protection."

"I just need to present our bona fides and then we're on, Shepard." There was a wary tone to Gatlin's voice now.

Shepard eyed the two men. They were toughs, and he got the impression that local constabulary might be a euphemism for local hoods. Whether they were or were not he was stuck with the situation and he understood Gatlin's desire to roll with it. It wasn't good form to question the integrity of your host.

"I'll be in the car," he said.

Gatlin nodded and when the two men parted, he and the greeter entered the interior.

Shepard felt the two men's eyes bore bullets into his back as he approached the 4Runner. He cracked open the rear passenger door and peered in.

"Stay in the car. I need to speak to Chad."

Millar opened her mouth to protest, but Shepard held up a finger.

"Gatlin's getting us on the guest list," he shrugged. "I'll be one minute, please. Stay here."

He closed the door and glanced over the roof at the swarm of growing pedestrians joining the protest and then the traffic, seeking the repetition of any particular car or motorcycle that passed and scanning the balconies and shop fronts for faces showing more than a passing interest in the new arrivals. Far from satisfied, he stalked towards Powell's vehicle.

"What's up?" said Powell, nodding in greeting. He had the window down and his elbow rested on the sill. Outward appearances showed a nonchalant passenger taking advantage of some fresh air, but Shepard could sense the SEAL was on a hair trigger.

"Christ knows," said Shepard, leaning against the door pillar. "Looks like the meet will be in the hotel on the corner. We're urban and exposed. For fuck's sake if Alfredi's been compromised, there could be fifty shooters blending in out here." Shepard straightened and again surveyed the street and the approach to the target building. "They could drive a car bomb right into the damn lobby."

"It's not great." Powell nodded in agreement.

"Gatlin isn't sweating it so I guess he trusts this lot," said Shepard, returning to lean against the car. "But I haven't survived this long without being wary of surprises. I don't know if the primary is here already, but I want you to stay out here with your eyes on stalks while Millar thrashes out the details."

"Roger that."

Shepard looked the SEAL in the eye

"If a bloody dog farts at you the wrong way, you put a bullet in it." Shepard screwed his face into a frown. "I mean it, Chad. The slightest whiff of trouble we're out of here, okay? And keep an eye on whatever is going on across there."

Shepard nodded towards the plaza and the chanting crowd. The SEAL gave a half cock of his head and a lopsided smile.

"Hooyah."

Any expectation that the hotels tired but once grandiose facade was masking an internal renovation more in keeping with a past heyday was sorely misplaced as the group, led by Dhusku's greeter, entered the lobby.

Shepard had only just returned to the 4Runner to update Millar on his plan for Powell to provide external security when Gatlin once again appeared on the hotel steps and beckoned them forward. Unsurprisingly to Shepard, the big hairy security guard made a show of closely shadowing him across the threshold.

Faux Persian runners dampened their footsteps across the marble floor. The tiles on each side of the patterned carpet were tired and cracked, and as they passed an empty reception counter in need of a re-varnish Shepard exchanged a look with Millar. The negotiator gave a solid nod in return, and he was glad to sense the business at hand and the familiarity of it had settled the tension she had been displaying outside.

A few fake potted plants which were ready to topple under the weight of the dust on their plastic leaves framed a stairwell leading down towards the function suites.

A duo of Dhusku's security led the way, followed by the greeter and Gatlin. Shepard and Millar had been sandwiched between the glowering gorilla and an anorexic guard with bad teeth and even worse personal hygiene. A short stroll along a carpeted corridor decked out with images of the hotel's glory days ended in a set of double doors which the lead guard tugged open.

"Welcome, welcome. My apologies for the cloak and

dagger. Please, come. Have a seat and a refreshment. Samira? Drinks." Dhimitar Dhusku ended the request with a snap of his fingers and wafted gesture towards a tense-looking middle-aged woman wearing a navy skirt suit who was hovering on the periphery of the room. The instruction sent her scurrying off.

Shepard appraised the former Romanian state security officer. He had softened with age but still cut an impressive and flamboyant figure. A neat salt and pepper beard did its best to hide a double chin and a mane of darker hair was fashionably cut and definitely aided by a decent dye. Dhusku buttoned up a crushed purple velvet dinner jacket as he stood to welcome his guests. His men, although discreetly positioned around the edge of the room, were all armed. One man Shepard noted had a Škorpion vz. 61 on a sling across his chest. The Czech made machine pistol had the stock folded over its body and as it was capable of firing more than eight hundred rounds a minute, it was the sort of weapon that could decimate a room in seconds.

"Carlton, a pleasure." Dhusku eased himself up from the head table and walked to embrace Gatlin, planting a hand on each shoulder and a kiss on each cheek.

"Good to see you, Dhimitar. Thanks for reaching out and for extending your hospitality."

"Nonsense, what kind of partners would we be if we could not assist in difficult times, eh?"

Dhusku bade the group to avail themselves of the seats arranged around a large round table more akin to a wedding party than discussions over the extraction of one of the world's most wanted. Shepard let Millar pass and eased her chair out. He remained standing off to one side.

"You may sit," said Dhusku, an eyebrow raised in amusement at Shepard's obvious discomfort.

"Thank you, sir," said Shepard with a small appreciative nod, but remained standing. "Mr Gatlin and Ms Millar are here to negotiate our exit with your other guest. I'm just here to observe and assist with your security and protection."

"You don't think I have enough guns, son."

"I'm sure your men are very capable, sir. It's just procedure." Shepard gave a tight smile and a dismissive shrug, hoping the Romanian would get the hint. Dhusku's face broke into a broad grin.

"Procedure, hah." He chuckled and slapped Gatlin on the arm as he took his seat again. "It amazes me that your two countries maintain their position in the world when you insist on all the red tape. I find situations like today pass much smoother when they are…" he paused, seeking diplomacy. "Not restricted by rules."

Shepard took a breath, a bit of the taut edge bleeding off now that the Romanian had taken no offence and seemed to be content to let him fade into the background. He took advantage of the passing of introductions and further pleasantries around the table to get a bearing on his surroundings.

The suite was on the large side and except for the table around which the group now sat, the rest of the furniture was pushed into the far right corner. Three sets of double doors framed by faded curtains led onto a broad veranda overlooking an arid hillside of rough vegetation and thickly planted thorns, the latter to curtail any more erosion to the steep slope that fell away to the trickle of a river and passing road beyond.

Shepard clenched his jaw. They were effectively boxed in. The only direct exit was that to the street, back out the way they had come. No doubt there were other means of egress in an emergency, perhaps a delivery entrance for the laundry and kitchens. He considered asking for a tour and then thought better of it. Powell was outside with a view of the square and was savvy enough to give fair warning of anything suspicious. In the end, he settled on the one positive, at least no one could attack from the rear. Not without climbing the dangerous and obstacle-strewn escarpment.

"There seems to be a degree of commotion going on, Dhimitar?" said Gatlin, accepting and thanking the returning waitress for the small glass of iced apple tea.

"It's nothing to worry about. Shop keeps and stallholders. They complain about corruption and then pay off local officials when they're fined for breaches of code or to shut down their close competitors. They want two bites of the cake and the cherry too. Imbeciles. Sometimes I hark for the old days." Dhusku sighed wistfully, but no one at the table commented. Shepard imagined how in Dhusku's mind the scene outside was ending with the security apparatus bulling in with tear-gas, batons and plastic bullets.

One of Dhusku's men discreetly interrupted, whispering in his boss's ear. The Romanian gave a nod and then obliging, his man retreated out the double entrance doors followed by Shepard's friendly gorilla. He took a step away and clicked his SELEX.

"Status?" he said. The earpiece warbled and then Powell's steady voice returned.

"Clear. The racket across the road is still going and the

traffic's backing up. I see two police vehicles caught in the jam. They haven't disembarked to try to clear it yet."

"Roger that."

Shepard, turning back, found himself under the scrutiny of Dhusku's airport greeter. Caught in the glance, the man gave a nod and then looked away.

"...to ensure that Khalid receives fair treatment. Even under the circumstances, I think he is putting a generous and credible offer on the table."

Dhusku sat back in his chair, having addressed an unheard question from Millar.

"Has he shared the contents of the drop?" said Millar.

Dhusku raised his palms and shook his head.

"No," he said emphatically. "And, I don't want to know. The less I know of the details, the better."

"Fair enough," said Millar.

A cough from the hallway drew all eyes and a second later, preceded by Dhusku's guard, came Khalid Alfredi and a second man who Shepard recognised as his personal security detail, Ramzy Joumaa.

The gorilla stayed in the doorway as the others approached. The big Jordanian eyed the room as he strode in, his contempt and the SIG Sauer P226 on his hip clear for all to see.

Alfredi himself seemed more coy and dressed for a casual business breakfast in black, skinny fit slacks and a white silk shirt, and brandishing nothing but a MacBook.

"Khalid. Please have a seat." Dhusku stood and welcomed the Egyptian with an embrace and kisses, gesturing to the empty seat to his right.

"This is Carlton Gatlin." Dhusku grinned. "He represents

Her Majesty's Secret Service, and this is Karen Millar." He waited a beat then whispered "CIA."

If Alfredi was perturbed by what he represented to the people around the table or for what he was about to do, he didn't look it. Shepard saw only a man with purpose and then he remembered just what kind of man the two spooks were ready to deal with.

"Mr Gatlin. Ms Millar. I understand Dhimitar has briefed you on the prerequisites. Given that you are here, can I assume we have an agreement?" said Alfredi, leaning forward to rest his elbows on the table.

Gatlin made to speak, but Millar beat him to the punch.

"Mr Alfredi, you're wanted internationally for terror-related and criminal charges, most recently for providing material support in the bombing of the Pera Palace hotel. We are here because you have presented a unique offer and as long as you can provide evidence you are in possession of intelligence equal to the grade of which you suggested to us through Mr Dhusku then we are authorised to negotiate terms, should that not be the case or you fail to fulfil your end of the bargain we are authorised to pursue a very different course."

Dhusku chuckled and Alfredi smiled at the case officer, both evidently amused by her candour.

"I'm glad you brought her, Carlton, she brings a refreshing note of clarity that is in contrast to some of the meetings I've had recently." Dhusku slapped the table.

As Gatlin broke into a smile, Millar remained stony faced and Shepard could see the tension in her posture. He had come to terms a long time ago that operating at the tip of the spear put him in direct contact with the worst humanity had to offer. More often than not, they were an enemy to be eliminated but, at times, those people would be allies in a common cause and he had accepted it. There was no doubt in his mind, Karen Millar was the woman to assess and bring in a whale like Alfredi. He had seen her confront warlords, terrorists and traffickers and those encounters tended to see the antagonists disappear into a very dark hole for the rest of their natural lives. This time though, it seemed the thought of actively assisting Khalid Alfredi escape justice was weighing on her and not for the first time Shepard himself wondered if accepting Alfredi's treasure trove in return for his liberty went one step too far over the blurred moral boundaries that too often framed their battlefield.

"Neptune. Neptune. Watchtower."

Alfredi was opening the laptop as Powell called over the SELEX. Shepard discreetly moved to answer.

"Neptune. Report."

"Ah, you might want to step out here. I'm seeing an escalation of local presence."

"For the protest?"

"Not sure. I've been getting the beady eye from a distance."

"Roger. Two minutes."

Powell doubled clicked his response and Shepard swore inwardly. If the protest was ramping up and the local police were moving in, getting Alfredi on the roads wasn't just going to be difficult, it might be impossible.

He looked to the table as Dhusku stood, straightened his jacket, and spoke.

"I shall let you conduct your business in private but you have my word that my men are outside and you are safe."

Shepard caught the Romanian's eye as he started towards the door flanked by his greeter and the second man from the front steps.

"Yes?"

"We may have a problem with our exit?"

Dhusku stopped mid-stride, waiting for an explanation.

"My colleague reports an increasing police presence."

Dhusku shrugged, a grin breaking his beard.

"It will do those troublemakers good to feel the weight of a stick."

"What if it's not that?"

A frown creased Dhusku's forehead.

"How confident are you this location has not been compromised?"

The frown deepened and Shepard could see he might just as well have pissed up his host's leg.

"You doubt the veracity of my assurances?" He shook his head in arrogant annoyance. "Listen to me. I wield the power and influence over those who govern this backwater. If there is any doubt over the security of this meeting, it's down to your people."

"The people in this room are the only ones who know we are here," said Shepard sharply. His hand snapped to his ear as the SELEX warbled.

"Skipper. We've guns on the ground."

"Shit—"

"What is it?" said Dhusku, noting the sudden change in Shepard's attitude and demeanour.

The SBS captain wheeled towards the table where Millar and Gatlin looked open mouthed at the screen Alfredi had turned to face them. Judging by their expressions, whatever he was offering, it looked to be golden.

"Karen!" said Shepard, loud enough to cut through her shock.

She opened her mouth to speak, then the first shots rang out in the hallway.

Chapter 6

The peril of panic exploded in the suite as a secondary expression of gunfire rang out, this time inside the building and very much closer. Dhusku's men surged out of the door towards the sound of intense shooting.

"Chad, sit-rep," barked Shepard into the SELEX, making a move towards the table and taking Millar by the elbow. Dhimitar Dhusku stood stranded between the negotiating parties and the door.

Alfredi's eyes bulged in his face as he snatched back the MacBook and Ramzy Joumaa snapped out his SIG and had aimed it at Gatlin.

More shots rang out as Powell responded breathlessly.

"Multiple contacts. Rifles and body armour. Definitely not cops…"

The rest of his words were drowned out by the crump of an explosion. Shepard felt the tremor of the pressure wave and dust filtered from the ceiling of the suite.

"Chad?"

"Roger…" The sound of steady and deliberate shots was audible now and not just confined to the comms. "Falling back through the lobby."

Alfredi was on his feet and the smug look of salvation had left his face.

"Put the gun down," said Shepard, jerking his head at the Jordanian.

"Fuck you!"

"You betrayed us," said Alfredi, his lips twisting in a sour expression of hate.

"This is nothing to do with us," said Millar, allowing Shepard to propel her up from the table. Gatlin remained frozen under the wavering aim of the Jordanian's pistol.

"If we had wanted you dead, dickhead, we would have just hit you with a precision airstrike," said Shepard.

"No, you need this—" said Alfredi.

"I couldn't give a shit about what's on that—"

"No. Shepard, we need it," said Millar.

"Seriously?"

Millar nodded. "Carlton?"

"She's right."

Shepard swore and looked around the room. Yells of panic and a barrage of gunfire from Dhusku's men rippled outside the door of the suite.

"Friendly." Powell's voice screamed over the SELEX. Shepard lunged forward and grabbed the host.

"Tell your fucking monkeys to hold fire, that's my man coming in. Hold fire, understand?"

Dhusku looked down to where Shepard's hand twisted the material of his jacket and then shouted an order. A few seconds later, Powell crashed through the double doors.

"Secure the doors. Grab the tables, brace the handles with the legs," ordered Shepard.

Dhusku gesticulated wildly at his three men who entered

the room behind Powell, the trio quickly dismantling the stored furniture, wedging thick wooden legs between the doors' brass handles.

"There's at least ten gunmen. Automatic rifles, grenades. They arrived in police cars."

"That's impossible," said Dhusku. "I would have been informed—"

The muffled scream of injury sounded from somewhere above.

"No point worrying about that now. We're blown, so it's time to go. I need a new way out," said Shepard. Dhusku looked at him blankly.

"What about me?" said Alfredi.

"You're coming too. Give her the laptop."

"Absolutely not."

"It's non-negotiable. Give her the laptop and you can hitch a ride with us, or you can keep it and try to talk your way out." Shepard jerked a thumb out towards the hallway. "Your friends are that way."

The rattle of rounds thudded into the doors.

"Dhimitar, that won't hold for long. We need to go," said Shepard.

Dhusku's greeter snapped from his shock at the sudden reversal of fortunes and pushed forward.

"This way. Follow me."

Shepard nodded at Millar, who gave a small jerk of acknowledgement.

"Khalid?"

"Okay," he said, offering across the MacBook to Millar.

"Are we on the same page here, brother?" Shepard moved forward to draw the aim and the angry glare of Joumaa.

"We are on the same page," answered Alfredi, reaching out a hand to press on Joumaa's forearm. The Jordanian lowered his weapon.

"Okay," said Shepard. "Chad, lead off. We're going to follow this fella and hope he knows where he's going…."

He let the rest of the sentence drift. They could all imagine the outcome if he didn't.

Dieter Kline dropped the 4TK laser sighting dot of his PP-2000 onto the chest of another target and let loose another burst of 9x19mm Parabellum rounds.

He barely felt the discharge recoil of the personal defence weapon, but ten metres away, his victim's face contorted in agony as the bullets slammed home.

A quick chopping gesture sent two of his men from cover and forward across the hotel reception area that now stank of cordite and brick dust. As the two hooded gunmen flanked the top of the stairway that led down to the lower levels and conference suites, he broke from cover himself, stepping over a corpse as he made his way across the bullet-riddled space to assemble with his men. A quick glance confirmed the area clear, and he ordered the descent.

The rats were in a hole under their feet, and it was time to flush them further into the trap. His reconnaissance of the hotel's blueprints and intelligence from his source had dictated his simple strategy of letting his prey gather together in the belly of the building in ignorance that their security measures were flawed from the start.

Kline, feeding back through his chain of reliable intermediaries, had managed to introduce doubt in the minds of Dhusku's security advisors, the notion successfully planted that the coastal compound was less secure than the city-based hotel site. For one, they had the opportunity to lock down the building and surrounding streets, had multiple routes of entry and escape rather than the one dirt road that led to the beachfront villa and miles of coastline to cover, and could utilise Dhusku's contacts in the local police. Unfortunately for the defenders, while all of that was true, it wasn't Dhusku who truly held sway over the local law enforcement. The consortium's reach went far and the coffers ran deep, and while the realisation of this would at first only come as they faced Kline's charging assault, the true scale wouldn't be clear to those at the hotel's gathering in the basement until they met the flanking manoeuvre the German's men were making to the rear.

Kline smiled. The attempts to slither to safety were futile. The operation to eliminate Alfredi and recover the material he had sought to buy his security and freedom with was going well; a slight hiccup as the American contractor on the door of the hotel realised the danger and called out about the approaching policemen had tipped his hand a little early, but his brazen full-frontal assault had snatched back the advantage.

The sound of furniture being dragged across floorboards and manhandled against door frames sounded down the corridor ahead and as he rounded the dog-leg and approached the conference suite, Kline unleashed a barrage at the closed doors thirty feet ahead. Muffled yells from inside offered the only response to his shots. Bodies lying outside, several men killed outright by gunfire and others succumbing to the shrapnel wounds of hand grenades.

Kline turned to the man nearest him and indicated the

pack slung across his chest.

"Breach the doors. They only have one route. Make sure they follow it and have no option of turning back."

The hooded head gave a nod, and then the man unslung the pack of explosive, and under cover of a comrade weapon, he moved to set up the breaching charge.

Kline dropped out his magazine, replacing it with a fresh clip, and turned to stalk back up to the reception floor. The layout of the building was ingrained in his head and as he mounted the top step, he called two more of his men to him and together they headed towards a second stairway to the rear interception point.

Shepard's attention wavered between Chad Powell's shoulder blades as the SEAL set a steady pace through the twisting corridors of the old hotel and the prickly feeling that clawed his gut when he shifted his gaze to Khalid Alfredi and his Jordanian muscle.

The fact that the big bodyguard had his weapon drawn at once set his nerves on edge while at the same time offered comfort they had one more gun in the fight. The glaring inconsistency in that train of thought and his distrust of the two men did nothing to damp down the tension of their flight. Somewhere behind the dull crump and thud of an explosion roared and the ground underfoot trembled.

Shepard reached out as Karen Millar stumbled against a row of metal and chipboard racks that ran along the edge of the small anteroom they were passing through, the glassware and china on the shelves clinking from the impact of both explosion and the spook's clumsy misstep. She clutched Alfredi's laptop close to her chest.

"What did he give you?" said Shepard, steering her into the next back of house corridor, with a nod to the computer.

Millar glanced back, her face blanched.

"Now's not the time," said Gatlin. The Englishman hurried along beside Millar. Ahead of them, Joumaa steered Alfredi in a not dissimilar fashion, the Egyptian's triceps swallowed in the man's big hand.

"Bullshit, it's not the time, we've been compromised and the QRF that is supposed to crowbar us out of a jam like this has no idea where we are. So tell me, Gatlin, how does that call to keep the meet dark make you feel now?"

Shepard's point was rammed home by the stutter of automatic gunfire behind them. Three paces ahead, Dhusku shot a glance back. There was anger and concern etched on his face and Shepard read in the man's eyes his regret at ever taking the Egyptian's call.

"It was the right call." Gatlin glared up at the taller soldier, his frustration that years of careful agent cultivation were burning down around his ears eclipsed by something else that Shepard couldn't pin down.

He caught Dhusku shooting another rapid glance and Millar shook her head and Shepard accepted the signal as an indication to drop the question, at least until he had moved them somewhere more secure.

Powell killed the pace a step and then with pistol up, swept around the next blind corner to clear the way ahead. He barked an affirmative and then marched on, the unlikely troop following and, having exited through a set of double swing doors, they found themselves in a fairly modern kitchen area.

"This leads to the back of the house of the restaurant and

lounge bars. Two minutes and we'll be in the rear delivery bay and then it's a short, covered walk to the street behind where we parked." Dhusku's greeter explained, moving around a galvanised service station. Powell followed, skirting the ovens and ducking under low extractor fans. Along the left side, a floor to ceiling bi-fold door opened out onto a veranda that overlooked the drop to the river and the road. Several stools and sand-filled metal buckets dotted with dead cigarette ends marked the spot out as a rest area for kitchen staff.

Shepard guided his charges along the centre aisle, and it seemed Dhusku had planned on a minor celebration following a successful transition of intelligence and secure travel for his friend. Pans simmered on stovetops and a large pot bubbled, Shepard spotting the unappetising sight of a broiling sheep's head and vegetables bubbling away unsupervised. Another crackle of gunfire somewhere in the building offered the unnecessary explanation for the current absence of the kitchen staff.

"There are two unmarked vans in the forecourt opposite the alley we will exit from. We take those and return on separate routes to the compound," said Dhusku, interrupting his observations. "Once we are en route I will call for reinforcements."

"These two and Chad go with you," said Shepard, indicating Millar and Gatlin. "Those two with me."

Dhusku nodded and Shepard shrugged off another glare of contempt from Ramzy Joumaa, no doubt at the suggestion they needed escorting.

Powell cut to the front, weaving between polished countertops and put the group on a trajectory for the exit to the service corridor that ran from the kitchen to the intermediate service area for the lounge bar and restaurant. As he stepped into the open tiled area leading to the door, the roar of automatic gunfire cut across their left flank.

Shepard grabbed Millar and Gatlin by the scruff of their shirt collars and shoved them to the ground and into cover.

As the two spooks struggled, his eyes snapped left to see three hooded men in police coveralls moving forward, TAR-21 bullpup assault rifles spitting 5.56mm NATO rounds on full auto across the space.

The greeter fell between the aisles, riddled from throat to hip by the ambush, and a second of Dhusku's men fell to his knees as he took a hit to the arm. Blood pooled across the once pristine floor and countertop as he raised his Škorpion machine pistol and sprayed blindly in the direction of the attackers.

The chime and clang of rounds ricocheting off metalwork added percussion to the bass of automatic gunfire filling the air.

Powell launched himself towards a row of refrigerators, cracking out return fire as he moved. His shots wounded one of the masked gunmen and drove a second to cover. As his clip emptied and he dropped to reload, Shepard popped above cover and lined up the USP's aiming dots, rapidly squeezing off rounds in an attempt to suppress the enemy advance and give Powell time to get his weapon back up in support.

A fusillade of more gunfire erupted from seven o'clock and he abandoned his targets, dropping below the countertop to where Millar and Gatlin huddled against the framework of kitchen units. Rounds sparked off equipment and storage as the two ambush teams pinned them down between overlapping fields of fire.

Shepard crabbed across and shouted into the ears of the two case officers.

"We have to move. They have superior positions and firepower and they're just going to walk all over us if we don't get to that exit—"

The familiar weighty thump of metal on metal and the sound of marbles rolling on glass sounded close by.

Shepard grabbed Millar and physically shoved her onto her face, piling himself on top of her and slapping her hand away as she reached for the dropped MacBook.

"Grenade!"

The detonation was deafening and the wash of heat and shrapnel lashed across Shepard's back and exposed neck like a swarm of angry wasps. When the shock wave abated, he struggled to his knees. His head swam and the smell of burning sulphur, clothing and flesh filled his nostrils. Fighting the tide of nausea rushing up from his stomach, he took in his immediate surroundings.

Gatlin was alive, but wouldn't be for much longer. A long sliver of metal had lacerated the left-hand side of his neck and his scalp and chest were peppered with shrapnel strikes and burns. As the spook's eyes struggled to focus behind a film of blood that ran from a vicious cut across his forehead, his breath came in shallower and shallower gasps.

A second dull clatter preceded the shattering explosion of another grenade at the other end of the kitchen and, taking a quick peek to survey the area, Shepard saw Powell slump back against his cover. The dark red smear that followed his fall told him all he needed about his friend's condition.

The rattle of gunfire pushed him back into cover, not that there was much more for him to see. The detonations had thrown a fog of dust into the air from cracked tiles and damaged ceilings and that added to the smoke from upended pans and the smouldering of cleaning cloths and dish towels billowing from the stoves.

A head wavered to his right above their cover and he snapped up his pistol as the barrel of the rifle tracked towards Millar. He got his shot off first and the hooded head snapped back, the mist of blood caught in the mask.

"Go!" he yelled.

Millar scrambled for the MacBook and yelped as a heavy boot struck her shoulder and another crack of automatic gunfire scythed across the kitchen. Khalid Alfredi loomed out of the intensifying smoke and lashed a second kick at Millar's hand. She cried out as he stomped on her wrist and then stooped to grab the laptop.

Shepard pushed up from the floor and moved to snatch at the Egyptian's free arm as Millar scrambled away, clutching her wrist, which he could see from a cursory glance was broken.

As Alfredi pulled himself free, Shepard launched forward again, shouldering him into the counter before sidestepping at the last second to fire two rounds into the chest of a rapidly approaching gunman. The impact rocked the man, but the strike was absorbed by his body armour and he fired an undisciplined burst which did little but add to the impact damage on the ceiling.

Shepard reached out a hand and snagged one of the bubbling pots, flinging the boiling contents into the face of the attacker. The figure dropped his weapon and writhed away, howling.

With the laptop clutched under one arm like a football, Alfredi palmed himself up and away. Shepard kicked out at his heels and he stumbled but managed to maintain his balance thanks to the support of his bodyguard. Joumaa pushed his charge behind him and levelled his weapon at Millar's chest and squeezed the trigger.

Shepard's backhand with the saucepan caught the pistol at the last second and sent the shot wide, his gun hand snapping his own weapon on target, but Joumaa was quick to react and snatched Shepard's wrist, pushing the weapon into the air.

The two men pirouetted in the aisle. A burst of submachine pistol nearby pushed the initial ambushers again into cover and gave Shepard some hope that at least one of Dhusku's men was still in the fight.

Joumaa kicked out at Shepard's legs, driving him back and trying to unbalance him over the countertop, his face streaked with soot and set into a snarl.

As the Jordanian connected with a vicious headbutt, Shepard drove a knee upwards into the man's groin, feeling a brief respite as his grip slackened. Taking the half-second advantage gained as the bigger man sucked in a breath, Shepard heaved left and then right, breaking out from under the Jordanian's bear hug to twist behind him.

He drove his heel into the back of Joumaa's left knee. Alfredi's head of security toppled to the left and Shepard used the momentum to slam the man's head against the gas rings of the still-burning stovetop.

Joumaa bellowed in pain as Shepard snatched him back up by the collar, leaving a strip of facial skin stuck to the hob.

Without remorse, Shepard put his weight behind a second smash into the blue flames. The impact and the shock knocked the Jordanian into unconsciousness and Shepard let him slump to the ground.

"Can you move?"

Millar was pale. Her lips trembled, and she flinched under the onslaught of another barrage of bullets.

"I think my arm's broken?"

"As long as it's not your legs. Come on," said Shepard.

He half pushed and half carried Millar along the aisle towards where Dhusku and the last of his men fended off the flanking attackers. There was no sign of the Egyptian.

"Dhimitar, where is Alfredi?"

"He ran," Dhusku pointed through the swirling smoke towards the exit doors. "Crazy bastard is making a run for the cars."

"Cover us to the corridor and then I'll cover you," said Shepard.

Dhusku's smile was tired and pained. It was then that Shepard saw the dark wedge ruining his dinner jacket. The bloodstain ran from his armpit to his ribs.

"I think my running days are behind me. Where is Carlton?"

Shepard shook his head, and the Romanian nodded sadly. "Miss Millar. I'm sorry I failed in my promise to protect your meeting."

"I think we were destined to fail," she answered cryptically.

A burst of gunfire sparked around them, much too close for comfort.

"Karen, we go in three."

Millar nodded.

Shepard put his hand on Dhusku's shoulder and squeezed. The old state security officer placed his bloodied palm on top, the gesture a silent parting of ways for the two soldiers.

Shepard twisted his head away as Dhusku's blood sprayed across his face. The rounds that ripped into the host narrowly missing him.

The muzzle flash of an assault rifle erupted five metres away in the next cooking section and, to his right, the flash was mirrored by another. The enemy had closed, and he saw two men leap over the counters to breach the rear.

Millar snatched glances left and right. Dhusku's man fell under a third well-aimed burst.

They were in the kill zone now and Shepard knew he only had seconds before he and Millar would be cut down.

A draught from the open veranda swirled the billowing smoke and he could see a broad-shouldered man barking orders over the chaos of the advancing figures.

He locked eyes with Shepard, then snapped up his PP-2000 and took aim.

There would be no prisoner trade. No quarter given.

The zip of rounds hit thin air as Shepard dropped and dragged Miller to the ground with him.

Twenty paces away, he saw the commander of the attackers pause over the prone figure of Joumaa and fire three shots into the Jordanian.

Two more followed into Gatlin's chest, but he suspected the spook was already dead.

"Run!"

Millar had a blank look. The shock of her broken arm, the savagery of the assault, and the imminent threat of death coiling around her.

"Run!" Shepard shoved her towards the veranda. As weapons swept to track the movement, he emptied what remained in the clip of his USP.

It was a minor but effective distraction, and the air zipped and hissed around him as weapons were swiftly re-targeted in his direction.

He crawled forward, clambering over Dhusku's corpse and plunged a hand under the open frame worktop nearest him, fingers snaking into the bowels of the appliances. His fingers touched and then gripped the stiff rubber hoses and, bracing both feet, he hauled the gas line feeding the row of stoves free.

Almost immediately, he was overwhelmed by the stink of the volatile mix of propane and butane as it hissed from the end of the ruptured tube.

The leader of the ambush swept his aim off target and twisted away, sensing what was about to happen.

Shepard flipped the hose up and onto the burning wreckage of the countertop, leapt to his feet and sprinted in pursuit of Millar.

As he reached her, the sensation of a huge inhalation sucking the oxygen from the space rushed over them.

Shepard shoved a hand in the small of her back and pressed her towards the open doors and the precipitous drop beyond.

A heartbeat later, the wash of heat and the ear-splitting explosion of igniting gas tore the kitchen off the back of the old hotel.

Chapter 7

The shovel-shaped rotor blades of the Merlin helicopter thumped a slow beat as the pilot bled power from the three Rolls-Royce Turbomeca engines and flared the nose of the aircraft on approach to the landing pad.

A hot thermal updraft rising from the baked tarmac gave the beast a nudge skyward, but the pilot adjusted her descent to compensate and the wheels hit the ground with the slightest of thuds.

Haley Adams killed the engines and flipped the switches that would engage the rotor brakes.

"One-One on the ground. I need medics over here now." The pilot's voice was calm as she spoke into her helmet mic. A CASE-EVAC under fire wasn't a new experience for the aviator, but it was the first in a long time where the precious cargo she was transporting to safety was a close personal friend.

On the cockpit mounted camera, she could see the aircrew and the soldier's comrades in the rear cabin rush to unfasten the gurneys carrying the casualties.

"Inbound to aircraft."

"Roger," said Adams, unclipping her belts and rising to assist the team in the rear. Through the cockpit window, sandwiched between the medical team in green battle dress uniform she could see a doctor in blue scrubs and a green plastic apron rush across the tarmac.

"Is he okay?" said Adams as she entered the cabin.

Mark Mills looked up. His features were pinched in concern but he nodded.

"Tough as driftwood."

Adams looked down at the blood-spattered and burned face below the oxygen mask. The blood pressure monitor and the patient's oxygen saturation levels told a different story.

Shepard's top had been cut off and his chest was dotted with sticky plastic discs as a corpsman monitored his dwindling vitals. His hair and beard were singed and his forehead, arms and shoulders were badly scratched and a large slash ran from clavicle to sternum. Shepard's lower half was covered by a foil blanket although his right leg was exposed, trousers cut to the hip and a large bandage and tourniquet wrapped around his thigh.

"What's the patient's status?" Mills took a step back from his captain as the doctor and two senior staff nurses from the trauma team leapt up the tailgate and approached the corpsman treating him.

"He's deteriorating. Airway is clear, but he's showing signs of smoke and heat inhalation. BP has been dropping on approach, currently eighty-four over fifty-two and he's tachycardic. Contusions and bruising consistent with a fall from height, left displaced clavicle, possible fracture of the anterior first and second rib and a gunshot wound to right thigh. No bone damage."

"Let's get him off here." The doctor pushed a lock of blonde hair from her face with the back of her gloved hand and shone a light in Shepard's eyes. The pupils were unresponsive.

"What's he had?"

"Supplementary oxygen and fluids when he came aboard. That's his second IV. TKO rate has been steady, and he's had thirty of morphine.

"Quick as you can, please," said the doctor, stepping back to allow the staff nurses to accept the IV bag from the corpsman and kick the brakes from the gurney. "We have a second casualty?"

Mills stepped forward from his position against the bulkhead to address the medic.

"She didn't make it, ma'am. Captain Shepard is the sole survivor."

Chapter 8

"So, do you still think the risk was worth it now?" David Yorke crushed a plastic coffee beaker and flung it towards a trash can, then wheeled and pointed an accusatory finger.

"I told you no good would come of this, Porter, but you took the bait. Hook, line and goddam sinker."

Christmas Porter for once had little fight left to summon a trademark acidic riposte.

She had crashed through the fire escape door and onto the tarmac just in time to see Shepard disappear into the trauma centre and one of the medical staff give a short shake of his head and pull the foil thermal sheet over Karen Millar's face.

"Do they think he's going to pull through?" said Yorke with an edge of pessimism.

"They didn't say much. He's pretty banged up," said Porter.

"It's a goddam—"

"Mister Yorke, take your seat." Duncan McPeak's flinty tone cut the tirade and left little room for argument, and Yorke did as he was told. Next to him, Giles Hammond looked shell shocked.

"Do we have an angle on just why this operation went so spectacularly wrong and more importantly, who was behind it?" said McPeak.

Christmas Porter swallowed. For a woman used to having access to wherever she wished, the firm resolve of the medical team in obstructing her entry to the trauma bay smarted, and although she'd threatened and bellowed with a little more vitriol than Shepard's comrades who were commanding a picket at the swing doors did, the major in charge let her voice fall on deaf ears.

"It went so wrong because Dhimitar Dhusku is a slippery SOB."

"Dhusku was an asset Carlton had cultivated for months," said Hammond, butting in to interrupt Yorke's continuing lambasting of the Romanian. "It makes no sense for him to be present if he intended to orchestrate an attack of this magnitude."

"The bastard was that arrogant he would never have anticipated he would die for harbouring Khalid."

"He wouldn't have given him up," snapped Hammond.

"Giles, are you for real? As soon as he caught wind the Egyptian was ripping off his paymasters, he would have been on the phone to somebody. I just don't know why he didn't put a bullet in him himself." Yorke threw two palms up and Hammond shook his head in exasperation.

"Dhusku was playing the long game," he protested. "In the name of God, he owned half the construction contracts in the country and with his background and our investment, he was riding the wave to high office. I've just lost a potential high-value government source in a region that's quickly becoming the frontline of a new cold war."

Porter felt her head begin to bang with a dull throb of tension and pain. She reached out to take up a beaker of water and they all saw her hand shake but made no comment as she took a sip and composed herself.

"We knew there was a possibility that Alfredi would be a target, but we've had no chatter to suggest Dhusku was involved or how the attackers knew of the location, especially as the primary location changed en route," she said. "It was fortunate we were able to intercept the GPS on the vehicles when they didn't arrive at the compound."

"Mister Hammond, I understand your man was Dhusku's handler and he was to be instrumental to a successful outcome but have you any thoughts on why he didn't call in the change of status and cost us hours in supporting our people?" said McPeak. He leaned on his elbows and surveyed the drone footage of the burning hotel and mob gathered outside on the large display monitor that dominated the rear wall of the box. Two police cars sat abandoned behind a line of SUV's and a further column of vehicles with blues and twos illuminated formed a barricade at the end of the street as two fire appliances poured water on the crippled structure's roof in an attempt to stop the fire spreading to adjoining premises. As the aircraft banked and took another pass, its onboard reconnaissance pod captured soot and flames billowing from a gaping hole to the rear.

"Mister Hammond?" said McPeak, the moment's silence stretching out as Hammond removed his jacket and cricked his neck.

"Operational security?" It was evident he wasn't sure if he believed it himself. "I think it's poor form blaming a dead man for this. Carlton Gatlin was a decorated officer. Your man was in charge of security? Why did he not call it in? Why is he the only one left alive?"

So far silent and sitting rigid but composed to the right of Colonel McPeak, Major John Canning sat forward to address the SIS officer.

"I have no doubt Captain Shepard would have made his concerns crystal clear and if he makes it through the next twenty-four hours, he will give us clarity on the decision making at the time. For your own health, I'd suggest you place your accusations elsewhere because strapped to a hospital bed or not, Tom Shepard is not one to tolerate the failure of others being kicked down the chain of command."

"It's a hell of a coincidence that—"

"This isn't the time to be at each other throats gentlemen," said McPeak, slapping down the internal dissent. "We've just suffered a serious loss of personnel and need to come together to find out who was behind it and what has happened to our intel. Miss Porter?"

"I have local assets on the ground but as yet no confirmation there were any other survivors."

"Khalid Alfredi included?"

"We've no information on Alfredi or if the intel he was offering was recovered or destroyed."

McPeak stood and paced around the table to stand by the monitor showing the circling drone imagery and alongside the others showing ground imagery and photographs from the recovery team and the developing picture from Porter's assets and local contacts now on site.

"This leaked from somewhere. Most likely through Dhusku's people or even from someone close to Alfredi, but equally, we need to ensure it didn't come from any of our partners or agencies." McPeak levelled a steely gaze around the table.

"Let's pray Captain Shepard recovers to deliver us his assessment but in the meantime I want every one of you to put any differences aside and be working hand in glove to get me a lead on who murdered our people so I can drop the fucking hand of God down on them."

Chapter 9

"Cara?"

"You're awake then, sleepyhead?" The woman's auburn hair tumbled against his cheek as she leaned in to kiss his forehead.

"Cara? I don't understand?"

"You're having a bad dream?" she said, then gave a small laugh, the sound a bright note in the gloom that hung around his head.

"Where's Tommy?"

"In time, pet. You'll see us all in good time. We love you."

A shrill wail cut off her words and Shepard heaved in a deep, shuddering breath that set off a series of sharp hacking coughs and the sensation of a parachute deploying jerked him from the horizontal.

His throat felt like he'd gargled glass and a weight sat on his chest. There was a brightness on the edge of his vision, but as he tried to focus, he couldn't piece anything together, the world in front of him no more than a coloured abstract. Voices blurred and as he twisted to tune in to the sounds, a bolt of pain shot through his neck and along the top of his chest.

He started as a hand touched his.

"Captain? Can you hear me?" The coloured abstract bloomed into a painful dancing brightness and he tried to reach out, but his arm was heavy and his hand connected to tubes. The jag of a needle nipping the back of his hand was just another of a hundred sensations of pain and discomfort.

"Captain?" prompted the voice.

"The woman? There was a woman in here."

"You're okay," the voice was soothing. Professional. "You're in hospital. You've taken a nasty bang to the head and you've a few other injuries we need to take care of, but you're going to be alright."

"Cara?" Memories began to tumble through Shepard's mind. A beautiful auburn woman, the gap-toothed grin of a little carbon copy and then the sensation of fear, an imagined sheet of flame. Of heat and pain and then a gaping emptiness.

"Karen?" he gasped, and the dancing light began to coalesce into a point. Behind the small pocket torch was a concerned face.

"Where's Karen?" he said.

"In time," said the woman, her words tipping him back to what he now knew was an uncomfortable dream as his subconscious duelled with the trauma of reality.

"All in good time. I'm Rachael McCormick. I'm your doctor." Shepard nodded slowly, but the movement sparked off a crippling headache.

Rachael McCormick put the torch back in the breast pocket of her blue scrubs and took a thermometer from the observation trolley beside the bed, clicking in a new earpiece she put it to Shepard's ear, noted the reading and then set about checking his blood pressure.

"How much do you remember?" she said. Her pale blue eyes regarded him with professional curiosity.

When he concentrated his gaze on his peripheral vision, the blur abated for a few moments and he saw she was fresh faced and her skin glowed from recent exposure to the sun, which had also accentuated the blonde highlights in her hair. The difference between her and Cara was stark. The doctor was lithe with a long neck and sharp, but pretty, features. Cara was… the sight and the feeling of her standing over him was still tangible and he shook away the thoughts and was rewarded with another overwhelming stab of pain.

A knot of professional impatience settled between McCormick's thin eyebrows.

"Unfortunately you won't be able to shake it off, captain."

"Tom."

"Okay, Tom it is. What's the last thing you remember?"

"We were compromised." He closed his eyes to battle the blur and thought back to the mission. "I jumped off a balcony."

McCormick nodded.

"Your injuries are consistent with that. You have soft tissue damage to your neck and arms and residual impact injuries to your head. That's likely what is affecting your vision. The scans suggest it will recover in time."

"How much time?" said Shepard abruptly. McCormick took a patient breath and smiled.

"Let's give it a day or two to start with." She placed her palm on his forearm and gave a supportive nod.

"You had a displaced clavicle which we've put back in position, a couple of cracked ribs and you were shot but, thankfully that was the least serious of your wounds. "

Shepard peered down at his leg, the wadded bandages now replaced by a large, square sticking plaster.

"How's Karen?" he said.

McCormick gripped his forearm, but before she could speak, there was a knock at the door. She didn't respond to his question, just maintained her eye contact and Shepard realised as he looked into the pale blue orbs it wasn't just concern for her patient but the sadness of a colleague. He knew then that he was the only one who had come back. Karen was just as dead as his beloved wife and son.

"You can quit anytime you know?"

Shepard opened his eyes and blinked away tears.

"Christ, Shepard. Are you okay?" Christmas Porter hurried to the bedside and leaned over the soldier. Her initial apprehension of what she would find had abated when she saw he was in one piece, but that reassurance dropped from the pit of her stomach like a stone when he turned his face to meet hers.

"Don't panic, Porter," he said, struggling to search for the bed controls. "My damn eyes are all over the place. Doc says it could be the bump to my head or the effects of the smoke."

Uncharacteristically, he reached out a hand took hers.

"I'm sorry about Karen," he said, the apology creaking in his throat.

"It wasn't your fault, Shepard."

"I didn't have any other choice."

"Hey, I know you, frogman. You'll have done what was needed. This isn't on you." Porter placed her free hand over his.

"It was a clusterfuck from the start," said Shepard,

flopping his head back on the pillow.

"Get some rest and we'll talk later. Here, Mark said you'd be looking for this?"

Porter took back her hand and reached inside her jacket pocket. The light from the bedside lamp caught the sheen of polished black beads and a sterling silver cross. She offered the item over and Shepard hesitantly reached out.

"He said it's your lucky charm. Guess he was right."

Shepard wrapped the beads around the first two fingers of his right hand and let the sparkle of the cross dance hypnotically in the lamp. The rosary had belonged to his wife. It had been a parting gift from her father. Her death had brought the item's true provenance into focus, but he had yet to part with it.

"Thanks, Porter." He gave the spook a tight nod which she returned, fully aware of the rosary's significance to him and the soldier's sad history.

"Don't fob me off here, Shepard, because I need to know the truth. How are you really?"

He puffed out his cheeks.

"I don't know whether I'm blown up or stuffed, mate."

"You do look like shit."

"I think I preferred Doctor Rachael's bedside manner."

Porter scowled and glanced back towards the door.

"She's too pretty for the likes of you, and she's too young."

"Don't be jealous, Porter. It's not a good look on you."

Porter snatched back her hand and swatted him.

"Don't flatter yourself, frogman."

They shared a look. The relationship between the two was complex and, at times, fraught with difficulty. The spook's world of grey and intrigue was often at odds with his world of orders and rigid convention despite the fact it was more often than not his team who were tasked with the practical aspects needed for her to achieve her results. The job had demanded they built a close and harmonious relationship, but likewise, on a personal level, they had moved beyond the professional to become close but never overstepped the invisible line beyond the platonic.

She knew Shepard wasn't ready to leave the memories of his wife and child and he wasn't sure he ever would be.

"Porter, there's something I need to tell you."

She caught his gaze roving towards the door and the ceiling.

"What is it?"

"Alfredi gave up something at the meet that had Karen and Gatlin spooked."

"Do you know what?"

"No, but after we jumped? When we were…"

Porter nodded for him to continue.

"She told me Alfredi set up a dead man's switch," he rubbed his eyes. "That if something happened to him during the transfer to safety information would be released."

"What information?"

"She didn't say, but the threat was implicit. If he was double-crossed and something happened to him, he was going to make sure the boats were left burning behind him."

Porter thought for a moment and then placed her hand over Shepard's chest.

"Get some rest. I'll have a think about that."

"Gatlin didn't call in the relocation? How did you find us?"

Porter leaned in and gave him a peck on the cheek.

"You love me because I'm mysterious, Shepard. Don't ruin

it by asking me to reveal my secrets."

He gave a short shake of his head and sighed, sinking back into his pillows, the monitors beside him humming and bleeping a lullaby.

"I'll see you tomorrow," said Porter, but she knew by the change in his breathing he had succumbed to the pain relief or the trauma.

Watching him for a few moments she let her mind turn over why Alfredi would need a failsafe and if whatever had been revealed to Miller and Gatlin might well have some bearing on why everyone who had come into contact with the information, save the man lying in the bed beside her, was dead.

Chapter 10

Dieter Kline turned the laptop so that the other men on the call could better see the man who was shackled to the rough concrete wall.

Condensation fizzed on a single bare electric lightbulb hanging from the ceiling, which illuminated a rudimentary table consisting of two sawhorses and some planks of oily timber.

"Well done, Kline," said the Englishman.

Dieter didn't respond. He stood impassively with his arms crossed staring at the prisoner.

"Has he revealed the location of the duplicate yet?" The man in chains jerked on hearing the question. The dull grunts accompanying his efforts to free himself proved futile.

Kline picked up a cattle prod from the rough surface, took the four steps needed to be within striking range and prodded the vicious prongs into the prisoner's chest.

The wicked crackle of voltage and blue sparks erupted as he depressed the trigger and the man jerked wildly, his protests and screams dampened by the rubber ball-gag wedged in his mouth.

"I haven't asked him yet," said Kline in reply. He turned back to the screen and put the cattle prod down. "You wished me to deliver a message. My guest will come to understand that there is no hope left, for himself and for those who he believes his silence can protect." Kline gave a disgusted sneer at the half-naked figure struggling to keep balance on his tiptoes.

"His death will serve as an example to anyone else who thinks to steal from you."

The expression of the man who resided in the top right corner of the screen gave a reptilian smile of approval which was matched in intensity by an Asiatic woman displayed in the square below him.

"Carry on, Dieter. I expect the recovery of that data drive to be expedited before it can be seized and our source compromised."

Kline nodded and picked up a set of bolt cutters from the bench. The sight of the tool set the prisoner on another terrified dance to free himself from his irons.

"I'll notify you when he tells me where it is."

"Very good. Have our statement and the video distributed to the usual channels when you're finished with him."

"Consider it done."

The heads on screen each nodded and Kline closed the lid and turned to face Khalid Alfredi.

"Stealing the money was idiotic, Khalid, but thinking you could slip into obscurity by trading secrets was arrogance beyond compare."

Kline let the heavy jaws of the bolt cutters scrape across the floor as he walked towards the squirming Egyptian.

In the chaos of the assault on Dhusku's hotel, Alfredi's selfish dash for the exfiltration rendezvous and freedom was crushed when he found Kline had been aware of the escape plan and had already overpowered the drivers. Any intention of regrouping and finding another way to reach out for support in return for the intelligence he held on both the terror factions he worked with and the consortium disappeared as he was hooded and bundled into the back of a waiting Nissan van.

Kline paused in front of the writhing Egyptian and made a show of easing the cutter's jaws open and closed.

"You aren't going to run anywhere ever again, Khalid, but I promise that if you tell me what I need to know, I'll make the end swift."

Alfredi shook his head from side to side. Snot and spittle coated his chin and chest. Kline reached out and pulled the gag down.

The Egyptian sucked in great lungfuls of the fetid underground air.

"I can't tell you what isn't true," he wailed.

"Where is the hard drive?" said Kline.

"There is no—"

Alfredi's scream was inhuman as Kline closed the blades of the bolt cutters on his right big toe. The digit bounced free as the German tapped the tool against the rough concrete floor.

"Don't insult my intelligence, Khalid. I have your laptop. I have had people interrogate the registry, and you duplicated a file in Sozopol. It wasn't at the house or on your boat. So who has it?"

"I—"

Kline snipped off the second toe, and the Egyptian

convulsed, his disfigured foot leaving arcs of bright blood and he slipped on the pool in an effort to take the weight off his wrists.

Kline placed his boot on Alfredi's bare foot, forcing it flat to the floor before placing the jaws above the knuckle of his next toe.

"Where?" he growled into the weeping face, slowly squeezing the cutter's handles together.

Chapter 11

Shepard dabbed a trickle of sweat from his throat with his good hand. The other had been bound across his chest in a dark blue sling by Rachael McCormick to immobilise and support the arm and shoulder affected by his displaced and now reset clavicle. A dark bruise peeked above the collar of a white crew-neck tee shirt and the only other obvious sign of the injury was the flicker of tension in his temple when he turned his head too suddenly to one side. Thankfully, his vision had returned, and he had managed to leave his bed.

The flesh wound to his leg had left it feeling dead, but he was able to assuage the doctor's concerns regarding it, the smoke damage to his lungs and his overall well-being, and by completing a mild treadmill stress test.

McCormick had sat quietly, albeit with a knot of concentration between her brows as the physio strapped on an electrocardiogram and oxygen monitor before conducting the assessment that would be the first test in getting back on the active roster.

Shepard had been surprised at the level of exertion he felt

as the treadmill incline increased. His leg throbbed, as did the bruise on his collarbone and the hundred other grazes that scuffed his body. A trickle of sweat crept from his brow and stung a cut below his eye and all the while, his heart ratcheted up to a level beyond where it should have been given the relative ease of the exercise. In the end though, his heart rate, monitored blood flow and oxygen levels scraped across the threshold requirement.

"You did good, all things considered," said McCormick as she walked beside him along one of the facility's stark white corridors.

"Who are you kidding, doc? I was like an old man." Shepard frowned, all too aware of what he had come through and how fortunate he was. A familiar face greeted them as they approached the door to his room.

"It has been said that you're no spring chicken." Christmas Porter rose from a visitor's chair and gave them both a nod. "I hope he's behaving himself, doc?"

"He's been fine," said McCormick with a smile. Shepard found himself returning it, grateful for the doctor's support and patience.

"Give it another day or two and you'll be requesting a transfer. Mr Shepard doesn't do boredom."

"Who says I'm bored, Porter?"

Porter bit back a grin, and Rachael McCormick blushed.

"I'm just saying I know what you boys are like without your toys. Do you mind if I borrow him, doc?"

"He should be taking it easy?" said McCormick, a flicker of concern for her patient creeping into her tone.

"I'll look after him. Promise. It's just a chat."

McCormick looked like she might argue the point, but in

the end, nodded.

"I'm going off shift, Tom. I'll see you in the morning."

Shepard gave her a nod, ignoring the look Porter was failing to mask.

"You can be a dick sometimes," he said as they headed along another bland clinical corridor.

"See you in the morning, Tom..." Porter mimed putting two fingers down her throat and then set a serious look on him and sniffed.

"Has she given you a bed bath yet?"

"Piss off, Porter."

The spook laughed and Shepard couldn't help but give a wry grin at her ragging. It felt good to act normal even if he didn't feel it yet.

Up ahead, a uniformed corporal barred the way.

"What's the craic, Porter?" He noted the stiff nod the corporal gave the intelligence officer and knew instinctively something was coming.

"Routine. You know the score," she replied, turning to face him and laying a palm on his good arm. "Take it easy in there. For me."

Shepard squinted down at her and noticed the frayed edges. The eye drops were doing their best, but he could see the sleeplessness and agitation. His friend was strung out and reading between the lines, she was fighting on more than one front.

At once familiar feelings of guilt arose. Regret at being out of service, at being unable to help her and the team uncover how they were compromised and by whom, and then the worst realisation; that he was the sole survivor, and she wasn't just fighting to find the truth behind what happened, she was fighting to ensure the blame didn't fall on him.

Shepard had never been in the room, but its purpose was familiar. He had escorted hundreds of high-value targets into similar, albeit most had not been quite as salubrious, if cracked off-white floor and wall tiles and yellowing grout could be described as such.

He offered a nod of thanks to the corporal who pulled out the chair next to the bolted-down metal table and figured it was some sort of karma.

His escort exited without a word.

The minutes passed in silence and there was little in the room to offer distraction beyond the crazy cracks and the single unblinking eye of a CCTV camera, which he did his best to studiously ignore. A single fluorescent strip light glared overhead and was reflected in the scratched and pitted surface of the table. He sat straight-backed and tried to find a position which offered as much comfort as his bruised body allowed and maintained his focus on the overhead lamp's reflection until his vision blurred at the edges and he felt the sudden phantom heat of the kitchen explosion rise up his neck.

The click of the door unlocking drew him away from his meditations. The still unsmiling corporal held the door for a harried-looking gentleman of perhaps sixty and then closed it with parade proficiency.

"Pardon my tardiness, Mr Shepard." The man dropped a briefcase against the leg of the table and made a meal of sitting and adjusting his chair, crossing then uncrossing his legs before settling both feet flat. One leg jutted around the edge of the table and he hitched up his suit trousers to reveal tasteful navy blue socks and a sliver of pasty leg.

"Captain," said Shepard.

"I'm sorry?" His visitor prodded spectacles back up his nose and frowned through the thick lenses, looking much like a mole as he arranged the contents of his briefcase in front of himself.

"Captain Tom Shepard."

"Ah, yes. Quite. This," he waved an airy hand around in fluffing gesture. "Is a medical facility so we try to offer a little informality. Is it okay if I call you Tom?"

Shepard gave a slight jerk of his chin.

"I'm Doctor Watson."

"You're a long way from Baker Street, doc."

Watson gave a small huff of amusement and a patient smile.

"It's not the first time I've heard that from someone like you."

"Someone like me?"

"The blade. The finger behind the trigger. The blunt instrument."

Shepard met Watson's impassive gaze.

"Sticks and stones, doc."

Watson took a handkerchief from his pocket and removed his glasses and gave them a brisk buff. When he replaced them, he slid an A4 page from his stack. He smoothed out the page before he spoke.

"Good to see the bump to your head hasn't robbed you of your sense of humour."

Shepard gave a wry smile and a minuscule shake of his head and Watson continued.

"Your recent X-rays show the damage to your ribs and

collar bone haven't deteriorated and there are no other broken bones or injuries deemed serious enough to delay your full recovery. There are some significant contusions and lacerations on your right-hand side, and the risk of infection remains with the bullet wound on your thigh. Doctor McCormick contests antibiotics and treatment should nullify most of the associated long-term risks."

As he spoke, Watson trailed a finger along the page to mark his place.

"How's the vision?"

"Crystal," said Shepard.

Watson had produced a pen from his briefcase and scribbled a note in the margin.

"You're a man of few words, Tom."

"You haven't asked me anything?"

"I'd expect a man in your position to have a lot of questions," said Watson.

"And you'd be the person to answer them?" Shepard raised an eyebrow sceptically.

"Probably not," said Watson. "But I'm here to assess how well you are coping with the non-physical so we can get you back to duty and in front of the people who will be able to assist you."

"You need to make sure my brain wasn't scrambled in the fall."

"More so to ensure that the trauma of losing your entire team is addressed before it has a detrimental effect on you."

"Shit happens, doc."

Watson gave a small sigh and frowned.

"I understand the display of machismo, Tom, but you've not had an easy run over the last while. The last thing our superiors want is to send men with burnout into high-pressure situations brandishing weapons."

"You mean you're here to reassure them I'm not a weak link?"

"I'm here to, in the first instance, ensure you are fit, and if you prove yourself the weak link, as you put it, I won't hesitate to report that up the chain of command."

Shepard understood the man was doing his job but knowing there was potential for a career-ending line to be drawn under his last, failed, mission, combined with the sudden pressure to perform despite being hampered by the effect of his injuries and medication suddenly made him weary. He closed his eyes and took a breath. When he opened them he refocused on the floor, following the cracks to a drain that was set off-centre; caught in the wire grid was a chunk of chalk-like stone. To the untrained eye, it may have been a piece of loose grout that had failed to wash away, but Shepard knew by looking it was a molar. He looked at Watson.

"What's it to be inkblots or are you going to ask about my mother?"

Watson chuckled and sat back. His expression wasn't unkind, and he offered a small smile of what could have been reassurance or perhaps sympathy.

"Let's walk before we can run, shall we? I'll say a word and you respond with the first thing that comes to mind. So, for instance, I say black, you say?"

"Ops."

Watson gave nothing in response but a short twitch of his lips.

"Ireland."

"Complicated."

"Trident."

"Brotherhood."

"Mission."

"Compromised."

"Christmas."

Shepard paused and flicked his eyes to the camera.

"Present."

"Cara."

Shepard couldn't help but jolt as Watson enunciated his wife's name. The recent morphine-addled dream and her very real though imagined presence rushed back to him, setting his central nervous system into overdrive. He could feel his blood pressure and breathing rate elevate and battled to control the nervous tic in his legs.

"Cara?" said Watson. The tone was questioning. He adjusted his spectacles, buying Shepard time while peering intently across and indulging the pretence the captain hadn't heard him the first time.

"Off-limits."

Watson gave a short nod and scratched a note on the paperwork. Shepard noted an almost imperceptible shift in Watson's manner. He guessed it was satisfaction that the evaluation was on the right track and him shutting down questions on his wife offered the shrink some vindication in the line of questioning.

Shepard cleared his throat and his mind, pushing away the face he would never touch again.

"Guard," he shouted. The sudden authoritative bark made Watson flinch.

"Captain, we aren't finished with this assessment yet?"

Shepard stood and looked at the sheets of neatly piled paperwork, then to the camera and then to Watson.

"If you think by dredging up memories of my dead family, you'll find a chink in the armour to exploit you're wrong, doc."

"That's not—"

Shepard leaned over the table.

"Will I get over the deaths of my wife and son? No. Not ever. Does my grief affect my ability to do my job? No. Not ever," he said, levelling his stare on the psychologist. "If I can compartmentalise my tragedy, then I can get over what happened to my team and that will go a lot quicker once I'm back doing what I do best."

"Killing?" said Watson.

"If that's what's needed."

"And what do those deaths represent? Are you subliminally playing out your own rage to ease the pain of your loss?"

Shepard pulled a face and shook his head.

"Those people make a choice, doc. If they come to a situation where they face men like me coming through the door, it's because they have chosen that path."

"Can you honestly say that pulling the trigger has had no impact on you?"

"If it's a choice between me and my team living and them dying? Then no."

Watson made to say more, but the door opened and Duncan McPeak entered.

"Sir," Shepard stood up from the table, taking attention.

"At ease, Captain. Doctor Watson, thanks for your time. Could you give us a moment?"

Watson murmured his acquiescence and hustled his papers together, rising awkwardly a second later to leave.

"I know you as a plain speaker, Captain," said McPeak, leaning back against the wall.

"I like to think so, sir."

"So without bullshitting me, how many yards have you lost?"

Shepard frowned at the question, uneasy at admitting how he felt.

"Doctor McCormick is doing a good job of getting me back in the game."

"That sounded like a swerve, Shepard."

"A couple of yards, sir. Nothing I can't get back."

McPeak nodded and stroked his chin in thought.

"That's what Doctor McCormick said."

Shepard felt a slight glimmer that being evasive and obtuse with Watson hadn't pissed off McPeak too much. The colonel pushed himself off the wall.

"Based on her sources and some of the intel we've recovered, Miss Porter is confident she can find me a lead on who hit that meeting. I'll sign off on this evaluation if you get your backside back to the medical bay and from tomorrow you up the rehab."

Shepard felt a leap of elation even as McPeak pointed a finger

"You follow McCormick's instruction to the letter and show me those yards, Shepard. Once Porter drops the bullseye Trident are wheels-up and I know by the look in your eyes, you'll want to be on that aircraft."

Chapter 12

Dieter Kline sipped a zero per cent alcohol pilsner and then reached down for a cigarette.

The street cafe was nestled on the edge of a busy harbour that overlooked the Bay of Trieste and offered stunning views of an azure Adriatic all the way across to the smudge of Italy's northeast coastline.

With his eyes hidden behind polarised Ray-Bans, he smiled at the waitress who passed by to remove the empty side plate by his elbow. His attention, however, remained on the front doors to the luxury apartment building across the street.

Khalid Alfredi had surprised him with his fortitude in withstanding the punishment he had meted out with the bolt cutters and a jerry can of paraffin. The Egyptian had maintained his ignorance through all ten toes and both thumbs before the slosh of fuel and the whump of heat crawling up his legs had induced a blood-curdling confession.

Kline crushed out the cigarette with a chuckle and took another swig of pilsner, enjoying the sun and soaking up the jovial atmosphere of the bustling marina.

Patience was a virtue of his and, as he considered many of the low dives and backwaters where he'd found himself shitting in a bag and surviving on cold rations while waiting for a target, this job was proving idyllic.

With Khalid's confession complete, Kline, as promised, ended the thief quickly. Within minutes of the fatal shot ringing out, the torture and execution footage was uploaded and being shared across the dark web, serving as a reminder and a grim warning as to what could be expected for those who considered crossing the consortium.

Two hours later, having cleansed the safe house and handed over the Egyptian's body for disposal, Kline was on a flight to Ajdovščina airport in Slovenia with his ultimate destination the old town of Izola where he would find Viktorija Radinski and Alfredi's duplicate dead man's switch files.

That had been a week ago now and each day Kline followed a similar routine, rising early to breakfast at one of the different cafes along the shoreline before passing the day and early evening in observation of the target apartment building. Any concern in missing the woman during his periods of absence was mitigated somewhat with the deposit of several thousand euros to keen-eyed waiters, marina staff and the concierge of the building itself.

Kline drained the last of the pilsner and held up the bottle to get his waitresses attention. He would have another and wait. He could afford to indulge in some downtime now Alfredi was dead, and he was confident in his assumption that Radinski was the type of woman who could only stay away from her palatial apartment for so long. Unfortunately for her, when she returned, he would be waiting.

Chapter 13

Undisclosed CIA Facility, Vlaska, Romania.

Shepard grunted as he hauled on the tongue of his boot and dressed the laces tight. Sitting back up, he rolled the kinks in his neck, taking great care not to push beyond the limits he had attained over the previous fortnight.

He caught a glimpse of himself in the mirror above the room's small hand basin and puffed out his cheeks.

"How are you feeling?"

Doctor Rachael McCormick entered through the open door brandishing a clipboard and a paper bag which she shook in his direction.

"Tired," admitted Shepard.

"Maybe your friend was right. Time takes no prisoners." McCormick's eyes twinkled in mirth as he bristled.

"It's not the miles on the clock, doc. It's the bumps on the road."

"Parting gift," she said, laughing.

Shepard stood, offering a warm smile, and a raised eyebrow.

"You shouldn't have," he said. "I haven't put you out of a

job have I?"

McCormick placed the bag of pain relief and antibiotics on the over-bed tray. To date, Shepard had only seen the woman in scrubs and surgical crocs, but today she looked dressed for success.

In a departure from the norm, her hair, which was usually tied up, hung to her shoulders in glamorous waves and she had applied a minimum of make-up. She took a silver pen from the inside of a smart charcoal jacket that twinned a knee-length pencil skirt and dark patent heels.

"It's going to take more than moving a few margins to get rid of me, Tom." McCormick put her neat signature along the bottom of the discharge papers and passed them over.

"Look doc, I can't thank you enough." McCormick waved away the gratitude.

"My job is to get you back on your feet and functional and from what I can see you're fit and you're capable." She gave him a reassuring nod and offered a palm to the air. "Stuck out here? Machines can miss calibration deadlines so I'm authorised to intervene when I think the tolerances are off." Shepard felt a surge of gratitude as she winked.

The last couple of weeks had been a boot camp of intense physio, active recovery and ever-increasing stress tests, the last of which, given the look on the operator's face, had not ended well. Dejected and feeling the weight of every year of service, Shepard had lain awake wondering if age and injury had finally robbed him of those crucial five yards. Needing air, he had risen and taken a walk. His trip through the silent corridors to a small external exercise space took him past the clinical offices where he unexpectedly overheard McCormick, McPeak, Major Canning and a couple of unknowns arguing his fate. His doctor's effusive support and personal assurance Shepard was fit for duty caught him off guard and he felt a swell in his throat.

Normally he treated injury as an inconvenience, irritated at time wasted and wallowing in the doldrums of ineffectiveness. Since the death of his wife and son, those depths of depression and the clouds of accompanying self-doubt that came with inaction had deepened but McCormick, to her eternal credit, had managed to nudge him to a place where he was now able to reframe it as time to recharge, rebuild and return stronger.

"What?" she said, noticing he had gone quiet and was staring. She blushed self-consciously and brushed down her skirt. "I've a meeting to convince our superiors on the benefits of scraping together another half million dollars from their budget to keep this facility staffed full time."

"I'm sure you'll knock them out with your pitch," said Shepard.

There was an awkward silence for a few moments between the two, and then McCormick cleared her throat.

"Don't come back too soon,"

Shepard huffed a laugh as she looked up at him from under her lashes.

"I promise when I do it will be on both feet."

Chapter 14

"Heads up, lads. Lazarus returns," announced Gash, beginning a slow handed round of applause for his returning captain.

The team had been billeted in an unused storage space off the main hangar and, as was the custom of special forces operators had managed to turn it into something resembling the bastard lovechild of a frat house and a sports bar.

A twin deck turntable pumped out the strains of Led Zeppelin and the smell of coffee and cooked bacon clung to the canvas wall that separated the pop-up bunks and a battered lawn table and chairs.

"Welcome back, chief," said Token, rising to his feet and making his way over to take Shepard's hand.

"Don't be shaking hands with that bloody Judas," shouted Mark Mills, a scowl and an angry finger wagged in Token's direction. "He's been telling anybody that will listen to him that your brains are scrambled eggs and giving odds of four to one you'd be back in a nappy."

Token gave a manic grin as he embraced Shepard.

"You should see how many of the bastards out there were taking me up on it too," he said.

Shepard shook his head, grateful to be welcomed back into the fold as though he had never left.

"Us, on the other hand, never had a doubt," said Mills, jerking his head at Gash.

"That's because you puddle pirates stick together like shite on a blanket," grunted Token. He spun around and marched quickly to a wonky set of counters. When he turned back, he was brandishing a steaming mug and a plate.

"Get your gob around that," he said. "Porter tells us that doctor bird has had you on matcha and wheatgrass smoothies for fuck's sake."

Shepard accepted the black coffee and the bacon sandwich. It was true to a degree that he had eaten clean since the mission and had stuck to water or electrolytes during the rehabilitation. For the most part, he felt much better for it but now with the smell of the bacon and the sight of the melting butter oozing from the bread in his hand, his stomach groaned and he took a savage bite.

"Were the three of you too busy to even bring me a bunch of grapes?" he said through mouthfuls.

"You were on a no visitors," said Gash, pushing in to peer at his captain as he demolished the sandwich, washing the last of it down with a swig of coffee. "Were you afraid one of us would put the scuppers on you and your new girlfriend?"

Shepard coughed, his eyes watering.

"Who—"

"Porter might be a spook, but she's crap at keeping secrets," grinned Token.

"Rachael and I…"

"Rachael is it?" said Mills, suddenly perking up to join in with his teammates' sledging.

"Captain Shepard?"

The voice cut out the taunts and the men of Trident all turned to what constituted the doorway to their lair.

"Colonel McPeak and Case Officer Porter request you and your men in the O-group in ten minutes?"

Shepard nodded and took a final swig of his coffee.

"No rest for the wicked," said Mills with a nod at his captain, the non-verbal gesture seeking the answer to the question none of the men would ask. Shepard gave a grim smile and returned the gesture, giving confirmation he was healed and ready.

"Game on," said Shepard.

"Jesus, he's only after his breakfast, Porter. Do you want to have him back in his hospital bed with chronic indigestion?" Gash pulled a horrified face as the spook pulled up the selection of grim images on the large-screen display monitor in the O-group briefing room.

Colonel McPeak sat in his usual spot with Major John Canning to his right. Shepard, Mills, Gash and Token took the arc of the table nearest the door and Porter stood alone at the front in control of the displays. Her intelligence colleagues were absent, both mired in the fallout of the failed operation. Giles Hammond to repatriate Gatlin to the UK and David Yorke to coordinate the operation between local assets and officials over the recovery of the rest of the victims from the wreckage of the Dhusku meet.

"These were taken yesterday," she said to the gathered group. "Local authorities are suggesting suicide. I'm inclined to believe it's something else."

The montage of scene photographs were graphic enough to

turn the stomach, but each of those gathered in the O-group briefing had seen much worse on the battlefields.

"Viktorija Radinski. Twenty-eight and associate of…" Porter paused and replaced one of the images of the woman's broken body with another of her lounging topless on the sundeck of a high-end yacht. Stood beside her in swim shorts and dripping from a dip in the azure blue waters of the Mediterranean was Khalid Alfredi.

"An online video has surfaced showing Khalid's torture and execution. The line of thought amongst those investigating Radinski's death is that she was either grief stricken or afraid that she would be next because of her links to the Egyptian."

"What a waste," said Token.

Any dignity in death that had already been stripped away by the gawking bystanders and cameramen was exacerbated by her nakedness. The Slovenian beauty lay where she had landed, on her back in a pool of her own blood at the foot of the eighteen-storey luxury apartment development that was registered as her address. Her limbs were twisted in unnatural angles and her dark hair fanned out amid the congealing blood.

"Tom, your relay from Karen that there was a dead man's switch was critical in identifying Radinski. We had believed the relationship was purely…" Porter paused as she sought a way to phrase it. "Professional." She selected another carousel of images showing the Slovenian dancing and indulging herself in bars and restaurants with tanned and smiling businessmen and a line-up of surgically enhanced beauties. "Radinski was a well-known face amongst the international socialites along the Adriatic and Mediterranean coasts. She was highlighted at one time as a potential source because of her links to foreign officials and other persons of interest who appropriated her services."

"Why was she not approached?" said McPeak, until now, like Major Canning, content to absorb the case officer's brief.

Porter pulled a face.

"Analysis deemed that any intel she delivered would have to be taken at risk. In short, she had friends in high places and we didn't have anything to persuade her. Bottom line, she couldn't be trusted if money was the motivation."

"Because she had easy access to the dollars." Gash whistled, "That's some boat." The final image showed a long-range snapshot of Radinski and a suitor exiting a helicopter that had set down on the aft deck of a huge superyacht.

"We've known for some time that Alfredi was a client of hers, but when I had the analysts dig back, it seems to have been a closer relationship than we thought. Khalid financed the apartment in Izola, and we've been able to track and isolate Radinski's movements over the last eighteen months. We know Khalid used a cut-out for some of his deals." Porter clicked up a map of Europe and North Africa with a half-dozen red dots added. "We can pinpoint Radinski as being in each of these places at least two weeks before an incident. We've received this from Turkish MİT showing her the week prior to the hotel bombing."

They all took in the contrasting photos of the vibrant Radinski strutting through the hotel lobby and her corpse. Colonel McPeak drained his coffee and set the cup down.

"Miss Porter, you're saying Radinski was murdered because she held this backup data?"

"That's my belief, sir."

"I know you don't work on hunches, so spit it out."

"Yes, sir."

Porter killed the images of Radinski and launched a new packet of intelligence results. The images and documents detailed her recent travels and aerial shots of the area around Dhusku's hotel in the immediate aftermath of the carnage. Several zoomed in on men leaving the burning building. One shot time-stamped twelve hours later showed a blond-haired male taken by airport security cameras. Porter pulled up a mugshot and biography.

"This man is Dieter Kline. Former German special forces. Post army career, he operated with the private military contractor Damocles in the Middle East and Afghanistan. More recently, we believe he has extended his remit as a gun for hire. He's been active in Sudan, Niger and South America."

"You think Kline was hired to hit Alfredi?" said McPeak

"I'm certain. This is another capture of Kline crossing the border the same week of the Sozopol attack. But this is more damning. When the Radinski angle came to light, I tasked my analysts to review all we could gather on public network CCTV in and around Izola. These are all of Kline in the week leading up to Radinski's death."

The selection showed the tall and tanned German for all intents and purposes enjoying a relaxing vacation in and around the residence of the recently deceased Radinski. It was too much of a coincidence.

"Do we have a twenty on him?" said McPeak.

Porter smiled and her fingers rattled across her keyboard.

"Dieter Kline boarded the motor yacht Petra yesterday afternoon. The boat's destination is logged as Venice, Italy.

Task Force Cipher has uncovered a booking under one of Kline's known aliases at The Palazzo Cavalieri."

She pulled up the exclusive hotel's picture from their website.

"I believe he's in Venice to hand over the drive," she said.

McPeak sat forward and gave Porter a nod.

"If that's the case, we need to move now and drop the noose around this bastard and whoever is pulling his strings."

Chapter 15

Twin V8 engines powered the luxury Riva Aquarama speedboat through the waters of the Bacino di San Marco in glorious afternoon sunshine. The sleek, ten-metre long, black and mahogany craft left a long winding wake as Gash pushed the three hundred and seventy horsepower engines to the limits and steered her through the seemingly endless flotilla of cruisers, yachts, day boats and water taxis.

The bow rode high in the water and Shepard who sat in the white, calf leather passenger seating behind Gash with Mark Mills, admired the view of the city and felt more refreshed than he had in several weeks as he felt the spray and tasted the salt of the water as they bounced across the trailing wakes.

The last time he had visited the City of Bridges had been a happier time, a lifetime ago when he and the then Cara Maguire were in the throes of young love. As he looked out at the looming dome of St Mark's Basilica he remembered the small back street bistro with its view of the soaring Campanile and the glow of Cara's smile as they shared a bottle of Pinot Grigio waiting for the sun to set. The image and sensation of his hallucination in the medical bay returned, but this time more than sadness, he felt peace.

As he turned his face to the sunshine, he nudged Mills and pointed towards the dock which was approaching at a rapid rate and to the large yacht bobbing on the azure waves, her name emblazoned on her hull in clear letters, 'The Petra'.

The captain and his sergeant were dressed in civilian clothes, Shepard in a loose white shirt and navy pants. Mills in a dark blue polo with a lambswool sweater draped across his shoulders and dress shorts. Both men exuded the confidence and appearance of the high rollers who were ferried daily from their yachts to enjoy the sights of the city.

Gash in white crew and linen pants looked every inch the experienced deckhand paid to make the return trips as many times as his clients wished.

The plan to confirm Kline had taken up his booking and then observe and intercept the parties meeting to hand over the drive recovered from Radinski had been thrashed out quickly, McPeak seeking authorisation for the incursion as Porter started moving local assets into place to secure sightlines and safe houses for the Trident team. It had surprisingly taken less than three hours to garner approvals and begin deployment.

Token had been dropped at the Lido di Venezia aerodrome along with one of the team snipers, Charlie Heath, to move west to the city and into an overwatch position covering the piazza outside the front of The Palazzo Cavalieri. The primary task was to observe the arrivals and match faces to anyone on the watch list supplied by Porter, and to cover Kline's epic suite which wrapped around the northeast corner of the exclusive hotel. Their eerie was a small and stuffy third-floor apartment accessed from one of the narrow streets feeding the piazza.

Gash cut the engines of the Riva and guided her one-handed towards the tourist dock, tossing the bowline to one of the waiting shoremen who wrapped it around a cleat. Leaping off the boat, the Welshman followed the expected routine, helping his guests to shore and accepting a tip from Shepard.

If anyone gave a second glance, they just saw another two men from a niche demographic eager to spend money in a city famed for its wealth and its once strategic position straddling east and west. Less than thirty seconds later, as the crowds flowed along the waterfront, any trace of the men's arrival had been erased.

Chapter 16

Dieter Kline clicked home the door to the safe and walked across the marble floor of his suite to collect a flute of Veuve Clicquot champagne.

His face and neck had been reddened by the rays of the sun on the trip across the Adriatic aboard The Petra and he opened the double balcony doors to sit in the shade offered by the striped awning where he could enjoy the view over the piazza below and the throngs of tourists and guides who passed in the baking sun with faces upturned to look on the baroque facade of the luxurious seven-star hotel.

The girl had been much less difficult to render talkative than Khalid and she had at once handed over the drive, offering assurances and oaths that she would say nothing of what had transpired. Dieter had thanked her and then thrown her to her death.

He wasn't worried about any fallout catching up with him; he was well protected by the consortium and by those who had sold their souls to the global group. The lavish sea palace that was The Petra was such a perk, and it surely made up for the days when his transport between operations was a bone-juddering ride in an old Land Rover or Toyota HiAce. He preferred this world.

The door to the suite was rapped once, followed by a further two short and professional taps, and he rose, knocking back the champagne. Pulling the double doors open, the butler assigned to him by the hotel dipped in a bow and ushered forward a white-jacketed and bow-tied waiter who wheeled a silver cart laden with stainless steel cloches and another bucket filled with ice and more champagne.

"*Grazi*," said Kline, heavily tipping both men as they made to leave.

"*Signore*," said the butler, bowing again in receipt of the tip. "You guest has advised he will be arriving at eight pm. Would you like refreshment served at, say, eight twenty?"

"*Perfetto*," said Kline, closing the door as the man once again bowed, then left.

He opened a few of the cloches and examined the plates, fresh fruit platters, seafood salads and a two-inch fillet mignon sheltered underneath. It was a feast, and he wasn't that hungry for it. His desire was to get the data stick out of his possession and into the hands of the man whose belligerence towards him had abated somewhat since the aborted attempt to take Alfredi in Sozopol. After the killing of Dhusku, and certainly since Kline had posted the gruesome video of Alfredi to the dark web, his contact's attitude which had previously simmered with contempt had mellowed.

Kline poured the last of the bottle of champagne into the flute and savoured a sip. He had warned the man that one day he would be back in a room with him, and he would ensure that the meeting left his contact with zero doubt that he may be the one to point and shoot but he was not a blind killer. He was a professional, an artisan, and he would be respected as such.

Kline took a glimpse towards the safe and its secure contents and silently hoped that one day the man who was coming to collect it would become surplus to requirements and that the consortium would require him to be retired as well.

"Standby, standby, standby. One-four. Eyes on Matterhorn."

Charlie Heath's voice was crisp over the net, identifying that he had Kline in his sights again, spotting the German through the optics of a Leupold VX-R riflescope from his perch a metre back from the sash window looking across the piazza. He wasn't waiting for a response so just continued to track the German's motion through his room.

Shepard set down his espresso and nodded to Mills' empty cup.

"Jesus, no," said Mills. "My back teeth are floating. Any more of that stuff and I'll be in the pisser the rest of the night."

Shepard laughed and signalled the waitress. He placed an order for another of the strong coffees and a selection of bruschetta and miniature prosciutto quiches.

"Making up for the hospital food, boss?"

"Just hungry."

Token and Heath had provided their two comrades with clear and precise updates over the course of the afternoon and as the sun dipped below the rooftops and the evening wore on, the objective moved to make sure they didn't lose the German or his expected contact.

Token had relocated to another cafe on the east side of the piazza where the hotel's guests could be dropped off by taxi boat or gondola. Shepard and Mills had the more direct view to the steps and the concierge booth where exclusive guests could be dropped off at the VIP entrance by armoured town car.

As Shepard wolfed down a bruschetta, he considered the plus side for the team going into the evening's operation. Kline was either supremely confident or just reckless as he had booked into and remained alone in his suite with no guards and no visitors, save the occasional delivery of booze and silver service. Should, as expected, Kline's handover make contact, the plan was simple, to apprehend both at gunpoint and recover the data drive.

Porter had provided documents identifying the team as members of The Carabinieri, the military wing of Italian law enforcement. As such, they would have the ability to bear arms and the status to enter and take Kline and anyone with him into custody. The downside came if they ran into the real thing and were identified as imposters.

Shepard put the thought out of his mind as Heath's voice cut back over the net.

"One-Four. Matterhorn is taking a call," he said.

Shepard pictured Kline through Heath's scope. A second later the German's voice drifted over the comms in a one-way conversation, captured by a parabolic microphone directed into his suite from Heath's eerie.

"*Ya, hallo?*"

"Moving, moving, moving. Target on his feet," Heath whispered over the voice on the line.

"*Yes, it is secure. Are you on time?*" Kline paused, a moment later he sounded surprised. "*Right now?*"

"Approaching balcony." Shepard acknowledged the report

with a double click of his mic. Across the piazza, he watched Kline step out onto the concrete viewpoint and lean on the rail.

"Da, I see you. I'll let the concierge know."

Before Kline had clicked the call closed, a set of headlight beams rounded the corner, leading a black Mercedes E-class up to the stand outside The Palazzo Cavalieri.

Shepard heard the ring of the phone and watched as the call was answered by the tall, lean figure manning the stand. He was too far away to hear the conversation, but he didn't need to.

Call ended and bedecked in livery, the concierge trotted down the steps as the vehicle's chauffeur stepped out to open the rear door.

As a figure stepped from the passenger side and a head appeared from the rear passenger seat, a second E-class rounded the corner and closed up the side of the first, cutting off clear sight of the men exiting. The passenger and rear doors of the second car opened and four men stepped out into the humid evening air. Each had shorn locks and their broad shoulders threatened to tear the seams of their hand-stitched Italian suits. Even from a distance, Shepard could tell they were muscle and knew they would be armed.

"All call signs this looks like us. Move to third phase," said Shepard.

He drained the last of his espresso and dropped enough euros to cover the bill alongside a healthy tip.

Mills eased through the tables and the two operators split as they began to walk across the piazza. To the right, Token drifted from his OP towards the front of the hotel. He had already made a booking for three in the restaurant, so access was no issue.

Shepard continued to walk left, keeping close to the stalls and shop fronts bordering the square. Mills cut directly across to follow Token into the lobby where he would standby.

The passenger of the first Mercedes motioned and said something to the quartet, and as they moved to follow their primary, the man turned to say something himself.

Shepard's heart skipped a beat, and he weaved under the cover of a souvenir stand, even though he was too far away and the crowds milling about in front of the grand old hotel offered enough cover to obfuscate his movements.

Once again he didn't hear what was said but he could read the gesture; you, you and you – with me.

Three of the burly bodyguards trailed in the man's wake as another effusive member of hotel staff met them at the huge revolving entrance door.

"All call signs. Neptune, be advised, switching to point of entry Bravo. The clock is set. Three minutes."

The team acknowledged, and Shepard quickened his pace to reach the side staff entrance. There was no way he could go through the front. Not now he had seen the face of the man due to meet Kline.

An ember of fury kindled in his gut with each step as flashbacks of the failed raid on Alfredi's villa and the fatally compromised meet in Albania distilled to a pinpoint rage. He used the emotion to focus, to harness his resolve and level his thoughts of retribution on the man it now seemed was behind that deadly double-cross.

Chapter 17

Shepard's language skills were rudimentary but a fierce expression and thrusting his Carabinieri identification into the face of the startled kitchen hand did the trick. As he left the youth in his wake, the exhaust vents of the extractors washed over him in a hot wave and he pulled aside the fire escape door and entered the riotous melting pot that was the hotel kitchens.

The space was a ballet of chaos. The clattering of knives and the clang of pots and pans competed with shouted instructions and calls for orders and service.

Shepard stalked confidently through the central aisle, palming away a sous chef who stepped into his path and then on towards the exit to the back of the house.

Each of the sections flowed in unison with the next, and the whole operation seemed to blend together in a blur of heat and noise. He was aware of eyes and mutterings as he passed through, but it wasn't the head chef or one of the other burly kitchen aides who moved to block his passage but a bespectacled waitress.

"Scusi, chi sei?" she said, marching forward to hold up a tiny palm and demanding identification. Shepard pulled his

ID.

"*Affari della polizia. Torna al lavoro,*" barked Shepard, instructing her to return to work, and that he was on police business.

The little woman looked like she would not be deterred, but on seeing the military police crest, she stepped aside. In his peripheral vision, Shepard caught her hurrying off. He spoke into the secure comms.

"All call signs. Double time. Be aware of internal security."

As he exited the kitchen, acknowledgement was relayed from each of his teammates.

"One-four, you remain all clear outside. No change. Matterhorn remains in situ and unaccompanied at this time."

Shepard hurried along the link corridor from the kitchen and turned right. The hotel layout had been memorised at the briefing. His route took him to a staircase that led down to a maintenance corridor. Halfway along, he paused at a tall metal cabinet secured with a coded padlock. He entered a five-digit code, and the lock opened.

He gave a tight smile. Porter had her moments and once again she had come through, her local contacts managing to fulfil their task of providing material support. On the bottom shelf of the cabinet lay a canvas bag. He quickly unzipped it and removed a Beretta PMX submachine pistol and several clips of ammunition. It wouldn't suffice in a protracted gun battle, but he was hoping it would do for show and encourage a quick surrender. Between the submachine pistol and the familiar weight of his Heckler and Koch USP 9, he was confident he had the tools to complete his mission.

Closing the cabinet, he walked to the end of the corridor and into a quiet stairwell, rising quickly up the floors to where he knew Kline's suite was located.

Token offered a broad grin to the concierge who responded by dipping his head in greeting and welcomed the guests.

It wasn't a reception the stocky SAS trooper was used to, but since he had visited a barber for a haircut and a wet shave and was resplendent in a grey two-piece suit and dark Russell and Bromley monk shoes, he cut a less terrifying figure than he might otherwise have.

Mills, on the other hand, although receiving a courteous welcome from the concierge, elicited wary stares from the two men left behind by the arrivals.

"*Bonasera*," he said. The big smile and poor attempt at accent turned the bodyguards' heads away. They had made their initial assessment, two rich pricks on the prowl for signorinas.

There wasn't much the SBS operator could do to soften the edges. At six three and as broad as a battleship he was imposing in any setting but as they walked into the lobby of The Palazzo Cavalieri where the patrons consisted of an affluent and cosmopolitan mix of mostly Caucasian and Asiatic guests, a big black man with the physique of a young Mike Tyson drew attention.

Token led the way across the marble floor, veering to the left towards a bank of lifts.

It was a short wait until the car arrived and they stepped in, riding in silence to the fourth floor where they exited to enter a bedroom corridor.

From the opposite end, a chambermaid pushed her trolley towards them, pausing outside a room to swipe herself in.

As Token and Mills approached, she removed several

bottles of water from a storage bin and, without glancing in their direction, disappeared into the room for turndown service.

Token paused at the cart as the comms clicked and Heath began his report.

"One-four. Standby, target on the move. Matterhorn is moving to the door."

Reaching into the dirty laundry cart Token pulled back a ball of Egyptian cotton sheets. Laid in the bottom amongst the washing was another selection of Christmas Porter's presents. Two more Beretta PMX's and clips of ammunition.

Both men took the submachine guns and folded away the stocks, hooking them onto the discreet shoulder harnesses they wore under their suit jackets.

As they moved towards the stairwell that led up to Kline's suite, the chambermaid exited the room and continued to push her cart along the corridor on her rounds.

"Dieter."

There was a smile on the man's face, but also a wariness behind it. Even with the three gorillas looming over his shoulder.

Kline didn't answer, instead, he pulled the door to the suite wide and turned away, walking back towards the salon.

"You two wait here. You come with me."

The bodyguards did as directed as their employer followed Kline across the reception hallway to the grand salon of the suite.

"Are you afraid I'll make good on my threat," said Kline. He poured a flute of champagne and offered it across.

David Yorke took the glass and raised a toast.

"He's as much for your protection as mine," he said.

Dieter slugged back his drink and chuckled.

"I can look after myself and if you want my advice, you could do with an upgrade." He aimed the glass at the broad man loitering in the doorway before he poured another drink. The big man had a thick neck and wide shoulders honed from hauling iron and he was either too stupid to understand the slight or too disinterested to care. Both mistakes in Kline's book.

"Do you have the drive?" said Yorke, cutting to the chase.

Kline nodded, offering a palm towards the plush upholstered sofa set in the centre of the room. On an antique nest of tables between sofa and a wing chair sat the data drive.

"So much trouble for such a simple device."

Kline settled into the upholstery and crossed his legs.

"Is it secure?" said Yorke.

"Do you mean have I opened it?"

Yorke perched on the edge of the chair, his eyes riveted on the data drive that could ruin him and put a huge hole in the consortium's coffers for years to come. He nodded and Kline thought for a second about just how much the American looked like a mongrel eyeing up kitchen scraps.

"It's secure," said Kline.

"You're sure?" Yorke asked again, too abruptly.

Kline savoured another sip of the champagne.

"If I wanted leverage on you, I wouldn't need of a copy that," he said. "There are plenty other ways to skin a cat."

Yorke snapped out of his stare and looked at the German, taking a sip from his own glass. His face soured, not at the taste, but the company.

"I won't apologise, Kline, you're a tool and a valuable one, but you need to remember your place."

Kline smiled at the continued belligerence of the man who believed he was above others.

The American was just another in a long line of faceless middlemen who thought they were indispensable and taking their cut by trading on their insider secrets. The consortium employed them by the boatload. Spooks; like Yorke, crooked bankers, corrupt businessmen, servile civil servants and politicians in the pocket. Each and all helped oil the wheels of a much larger machine, but equally, none would be missed if it came to it.

"I know my place," said Kline. "The question is, have you forgotten yours? Khalid got above himself and look what happened. It would serve you well not to make the same mistake."

Yorke blanched and tried to mask it with another sip of his drink.

"I know my place. Yes, and I know the benefits and insights my position brings to the table," he stammered. "You and I can agree to disagree on personality and on methods, but we have to find a path to continue working together."

"I've no problem with that as long as you understand, unlike your hirelings, I am a professional," said Kline, once again aiming his glass at the oblivious statue across the room.

"Can I have the drive?"

Kline eased across the sofa and picked up the black plastic storage device. He hefted its weight and let his stare settle on Yorke.

"What?" said Yorke. "Do you want me to beg?"

"I want you to understand I'm handing you your

freedom?"

Yorke held out a hand and Kline placed the device in his palm. The American looked down at the anonymous thing. Bland and blank, but brimming with a stockpile of secrets. Most corresponded to transactions and areas of operations in theatres around the globe. Registers of assets that sluiced wealth from the casinos of Macao to the offshore accounts in the Caymans, and, the most explosive and damaging to Yorke; those that related to his own hand in the global game. His decision to turn had been swift and his corruption immediate. He was a back door into counter-terror operations and the war on organised crime, a set of eyes and ears that were ever alert to the authorities who desperately battled to close down those lucrative trades thriving in a dark marketplace.

The external door to the suite was knocked.

Yorke's head snapped round at the sudden noise. Kline stood and passed across the bottle of Veuve Clicquot.

"Relax, I ordered refreshments. Let's seal the deal over some food and at least pretend to tolerate each other."

Yorke swallowed as he put the drive holding his involvement in the consortium's global dealings into his jacket pocket.

Kline breezed past the guard with a shake of his head and entered the lobby seeking two men, but only finding one.

Yorke's remaining gorillas thumbed the door catch and pulled the door open. The flush of the toilet in the bathroom told Kline where the second man had absconded to.

Kline swore at the ineptitude.

"Imbecile. Did you even check who it was first…?"

His complaints died in his throat as the bodyguard at the

door dropped like a felled tree.

The door to the suite swung open and the bovine features of the meathead inside crumpled in confusion at the scene in the hallway.

"Room service," said Shepard, flipping a bottle of Krug premium off the meal trolley and swinging it in a huge arcing uppercut at the man's jaw.

The heavy base of the bottle landed home with a dull thunk and the figure rocked back, comatose before he hit the tiles.

Shepard was through the door in a flash, pulling the Beretta PMX from under his jacket and bringing it to bear on the shocked figure of Dieter Kline stranded mid step in the lobby.

"Hands, hands, hands." Shepard dropped the aim point centre mass and flicked the barrel in the air to emphasise his instruction.

The surrounding air sizzled as incoming rounds erupted from an open archway to his right, the bullets zipping past his head to pepper the wall. The shots were as close to Kline as himself.

Shepard swore as he ducked, the simple smash and grab suddenly gone to shit.

Kline spun on his heel and ran, sprinting back into the main salon and heaving an ornate grandfather clock across the entrance.

Mills strode into the lobby, sighted his weapon and let loose a volley of his own.

The 9x19mm Parabellum rounds stitched along the antique wooden panelling. Splinters and brick dust bloomed from the impacts and drove the gunman back up the short hall.

Shepard took advantage and charged forward, sending a barrage through the arch as he passed, but the shooter had found cover in one of the rooms.

"Go!" shouted Mills.

Shepard nodded and moved, shouldering aside the toppled clock and sweeping into the ornate salon.

Two more gunshots struck the upright and the lintel of the door, a third shattering a stained glass panel inches from his face.

To his right, he spotted Kline manhandling David Yorke towards another link corridor that led to the master bedroom and a chef's kitchen.

His more pressing issue was the gunman blocking the route and adjusting his aim.

Shepard took a long slide across the marble floor, gathering up a Persian rug as he rolled behind the sofa set bisecting the salon.

Gunshots followed him and the material and filling of the seat puffed into the air as the round thwacked home.

"One-four. The call has gone out. Local authorities have been notified of shots fired. You need to move."

Heath's voice crackled on the network, the clarity dampened by another fusillade. Shepard heard the gunman's footsteps as he broke right to close the angle.

He popped up and squeezed off half a clip. The rounds destroyed the artefacts arranged on an elegant sideboard and shattering a large wall mounted mirror.

The gunman scrambled, seeking cover of his own, half falling through one of the adjoining doors in his attempt to reach safety.

"Have you sight of the primary?" said Shepard.

"Negative."

In the hallway, another round of gunfire was exchanged. Shepard heard Token's voice cut over the net. He and Mills were running and gunning to press home the advantage of having superior firepower on the first shielding gunman.

Moving from a crouch, Shepard darted for the balcony, the open doors offering cover and a different angle on the room.

As the seconds passed, he sensed the distance to reach Kline and Yorke was growing.

The gunman appeared to his right again, leaning out from the open doorway ahead, both hands steadying his pistol.

A tinkling of glass preceded the sonic zip as Heath's shot ripped across the piazza and into the room. The .338 Lapua Magnum round from his suppressed Stealth Recon Scout rifle hit the gunman in the sternum and he crumpled.

"You're clear. "

"Roger, moving," said Shepard, sprinting for the corridor where moments before Kline and Yorke had disappeared.

Outside in the streets, he could hear the toll of approaching sirens.

Chapter 18

Yorke was white. The abrupt interruption and sudden violence had left his face a sheet-white mask.

Kline held him by the collar and manhandled him along the bedroom corridor, wheeling left and then changing his mind and dragging him right and along the short link to the chef's kitchen, which seemed a better option. It had weapons for one, and a fire escape.

The German cursed himself for being lax, then gave a small chuckle as he bounced Yorke off the door frame and into the small private kitchen. He hadn't been lax; he had been arrogant.

"You need to get us out of here," stammered Yorke.

The drive in his pocket felt like an anchor dragging him down, but it was not as heavy as the cloak of fear that had shrouded him as he watched Shepard enter the salon. Ever since it had been confirmed that there had been a survivor from the hotel attack, anxiety had clawed at his gut. More so when he found out who exactly had managed to crawl from the burning wreckage. The tension had only increased when his attempt to muddy the waters had stalled and Major Canning had been succinct in explaining what Shepard might do when faced with carrying the can of failure.

Now here they were, both architect and executioner in the sights of Trident's illustrious captain.

The shooting from the salon ended abruptly, and he heard raised voices inside the suite and sirens outside.

"Get over there," snapped Kline, pushing him along the side of the kitchen island. The German slid a broad-bladed eight-inch chef's knife from the moulded block.

"Kline—"

"Shut up," hissed the German. Yorke flinched as he pushed past. The door from the kitchen to the escape stair was locked. Kline looked at the non-regulation chain and padlock wrapped around the crash bar and swore.

Yorke looked ill.

"Make yourself useful for fuck's sake." Kline jostled past the American again and began to pull open drawers, ransacking the contents for sign of a key.

Yorke followed suit, frantically searching round appliances and along the island's storage boxes and sills.

"Got it," announced Kline triumphantly. He darted to the door and wrestled with the chain and lock, dropping the freed hasp and thumping the crash bar.

The door swung open and the humid air of the piazza and the smell of the canal washed in.

"Go," he pushed Yorke through.

A gunshot struck the wall high and right.

"Stand down!" boomed Shepard, "Get away from the door."

Kline spun and launched the chef's knife.

Shepard dipped left to avoid the spinning blade and then brought his PMX up to re-target the German.

Footsteps clanged on the escape stairs.

Kline grabbed a blender and sent it arcing towards the Trident captain, then pivoted to snatch again at the knife block, his fingers wrapping around a six-inch boning blade.

Shepard batted the flying equipment away and again made to aim, but Kline was on him, slashing the blade at his face.

The glimmer of steel skimmed his eyes and as the backhand returned, Shepard parried with his weapon, driving the German's hand high.

Kline lashed out a punch with his free hand and Shepard again parried with his left before driving a heavy kick into the German's abdomen.

The mercenary had spotted it coming, the blow identified by experience and the cramped space, and he allowed momentum to take him towards the open door.

He swapped knife hands, again thrusting and slashing. Anything to keep his adversary from taking advantage of having superior weaponry.

Shepard bobbed and weaved, lurching back to avoid a particularly vicious slash across his throat.

The Beretta PMX was an excellent close combat weapon, but he couldn't bring it to bear under the rabid onslaught and reverted to using it as a defensive club.

The seconds were ticking away, the time mounting for the authorities to assemble and take control and for Yorke to disappear. He batted Kline's thrust wide left and then charged, barrelling into the German and taking them both through the open fire escape door and over the rail of the balcony.

They landed in a heavy crash on the iron grid of the landing below.

As Shepard righted himself he saw Yorke hit the ground floor and weave across a narrow footbridge that crossed the canal onto the piazza.

He didn't have time to concern himself as Yorke melted into the crowds of faces staring at the hotel and the approaching blue lights.

Kline launched himself forward, a flurry of elbows and knees driving blows into him. Shepard blocked as he could and rode the blows that he couldn't. Blood trickled from a cut on his chin and he felt the tightness of his previous injuries.

The German caught his lapels with both hands and threw a brutal headbutt that glanced off as Shepard twisted, the blow catching his shoulder as he lashed out with a sweep and then dragged his heel along the German's shin.

Kline's pressure faltered and Shepard threw a heavy fist into his opponent's solar plexus, pushing him off.

The blow knocked the breath from Kline and he lost balance, throwing himself backwards, pinwheeling to stay upright and fortuitous when, in finding his feet, he was beside the fallen PMX.

Still breathless, he stooped quickly and snatched the weapon up, sweeping the barrel towards Shepard.

A single shot rang out in the night, the muzzle flash and report echoing off the facade of The Palazzo Cavalieri.

Kline dropped the submachine gun and fell back against the escape railing.

Shepard stalked forward, USP 9 brandished in both hands.

"That one's for Chad Powell," he said.

Kline took a shuddering breath but felt the inhalation catch. There was a ragged hole in the left side of his chest. Deep under the muscle of his pectoral, the lung was perforated and the wet sucking of air sounded harsh in his ears.

Shepard levelled his weapon and pulled the trigger.

The impact caught Kline on the bridge of the nose, momentum flipping him back over the rail and into the air.

Shepard watched his body hit the black water of the canal.

"That one is for Karen Millar."

Chapter 19

The Black Sea Coast

The sleek profile of the 'The Bella Andrea' was silhouetted against the dying light of the day in a stunning anchorage off a coast of pristine beaches and exclusive villas.

David Yorke looked out from the swim deck of the elegant sixty-five-metre yacht towards the approaching tender with a more than a hint of trepidation. The azure blue was on the turn to raven black and the colour of the water matched his mood.

His flight from Venice had been blessed by luck but was not without incident. The relief of leaping from the small footbridge to be enveloped by the anonymous crowd of sightseers and rubberneckers who watched the chaos unfold as the blazing lights and sirens of the gendarmerie as they tore into the piazza was overwhelming. He hadn't looked back as he fled through the narrow streets to the water taxi dock.

It was then that things became heated as once aboard and transported across the bay to the dock at the *Stazione Marittima,* he realised then he had no means to pay and no means of communication. His pilot, having fallen foul all too often to the tourist's ploy had no intention of writing off the trip, and screeched in irritated Italian before calling for the polizia.

Lady Luck once again came to his aid when an octogenarian couple heard the commotion and recognising the plight of a countryman in need, paid the small fee to the boatman and offered a phone so he could make a call.

Effusive thanks waved away, Yorke had then been collected, transported to an apartment safe house for the night and then in the morning was dropped to a small provincial airport where a private plane waited on the tarmac to whisk him back across the Adriatic to *Aeroportul Tuzla* and then his waiting transfer brought him to the glossy teak decks of 'The Bella Andrea'.

The man approaching in the tender had more than a little to do with his escape and subsequent evasion from the authorities and a lot to do with the knot of fear in Yorke's gut.

As the tender skipped across the water, closing rapidly, he took a breath and steadied himself, taking a moment to look out across the bay where the last of the day's fun seekers raced a jet ski through the moored yachts and pleasure craft. The big Yamaha cut skilfully through the water, ridden by a woman, her hair catching the face of her male partner who sat behind her in the breeze.

A chorus of delighted laughter drifted on the sea breeze and Yorke wished the meeting was over and the data drive out of his hands so he could get back to seeking a crumb of their carefree revelry.

❖❖❖

"David."

"Welcome aboard," said Yorke, extending a hand in greeting and presenting a warm smile and then a palm up to the sun deck where a table was laid and a uniformed steward was poised to pour glasses of Castello di Cacchiano Chianti.

The Englishman shook Yorke's hand warmly and accepted the invitation to sit before he spoke.

"I trust you are well recovered from your shock?" he said.

Yorke nodded at the steward and waited as he poured before committing to a reply and only then after he had chinked glasses and sampled a sip of the Chianti, savouring the dark cherry palate and the clean strawberry aftertaste.

"I am, and again, thank you. I'm in your debt."

"You most certainly are," said the Englishman with no hint of irony or that he was in any way ready to make light of the support and effort it had taken to extract the American case officer. "The problem I'm faced with is, you are now damaged goods, old boy, so your ability to pay me back has been radically curtailed."

Yorke felt a sliver of ice cut through his bowels.

"Oh, for goodness sake, wipe the terror off your face. I've lost enough assets in the last couple of days not to be here to witness the death of another."

Yorke didn't speak. He regarded the Englishman's expression for anything less than total candour.

The Englishman represented the consortium, and the group was not well known for administering second, much less third, chances. The man's area of responsibility covered Eastern Europe and the Caucasus. His remit to administer the splinter groups and organisations working to fulfil the consortium's agenda in the region and ensure financial probity in those dealings and the fulfilment of the black market contracts.

"Do you have the device?"

Yorke snapped out of his daze, nodding stiffly and then moving awkwardly to retrieve the data drive from a box set on the deck table.

"There you go."

The Englishman gave an approving nod and then toasted his host.

"Thank you. It's been a concern that this amount of information has been floating about unchecked so seeing it secured offers a great deal of reassurance, which brings me to my offer."

Yorke hid his continued anxiety behind a swig of his wine, his Adam's apple bobbing as he swallowed and nodded for his guest to continue.

"Evidently, it was a significant breach which enabled the theft of this information. You are aware of the impact it could have had on operational capability and revenue streams should it have fallen into the wrong hands."

Yorke nodded his agreement with his face set into a serious frown.

"We believe a man of your skills could be the one to undertake a review and report your findings on any purge that needs to take place."

Yorke felt the first glimmer of redemption. He puffed out his cheeks, unsure how to respond.

"We might have lost your ability to operate on the inside, but we can still utilise your contacts and put your talents to other uses," explained the Englishman. He drained his wine, securing the drive in the pocket of his linen jacket.

"And my former colleagues?"

"You have fallen from the grid and into our protection, David. Dieter's death was unfortunate, but in retrieving this you have shown a degree of resourcefulness."

"Thank you," said Yorke.

"Your old life is behind you and any ties to it will be severed. We'll ensure any blowback from Venice falls on your old colleagues and make arrangements for you to receive a new legend."

Yorke felt his head swim, unsure if it was the booze or elation at escaping what he'd felt was an almost certain grim future, either on the periphery or at the bottom of the deep blue.

"Take a few days and think about what you'll need to get started," said the Englishman. He stood and gestured around the sun deck. "Enjoy the yacht until the end of the week and someone will be in touch with instructions."

Yorke took the offered hand, feeling his cheeks flush.

"Thank you. I mean it. Please pass on my gratitude."

The Englishman gave a curt nod, but he didn't reply. He turned and made his way back down from the exterior aft deck to the swim platform and the waiting tender.

Yorke walked to the gunwale, leaned over the polished chrome deck rail and watched the smaller boat leave, its running lights blinking as they shrank into the growing night.

He turned and found the steward exiting the sky lounge to clear the table but dismissed the man as he made to retrieve the Chianti.

"Leave it," said Yorke, a smile breaking his face and the tension of the last few weeks ebbing away as he began to contemplate a new life. "It's time to toast old comrades and new beginnings."

Chapter 20

The swim from the rocky outcrop that segregated a crescent of sandy shore from a slightly raised bank of marine grass and a long tarmac promenade took fifteen minutes.

In the months leading up to selection, Shepard would have covered the distance in half the time, and in the months and years afterwards, he had endured so much time immersed in the sea it was a wonder he hadn't grown gills and webbed feet.

SBS. Special Boat Service. As he bobbed in the black water with only his eyes and the top of his head visible above the surface, Shepard reflected on how much more time he seemed to spend out of the vessels than in them.

The Royal Navy's elite had avoided the celebrity spotlight of their compatriots in the SAS over the years until their exploits battling insurgency in the rugged mountains and cities of Afghanistan and Iraq and fighting the scourge of piracy in the Arabian Sea had illustrated a ferocity and professionalism in getting the job done.

Shepard sculled towards the hull of 'The Bella Andrea' with his senses tuned for any sign of life, ducking the anchor chain and quietly moving along the port side, rounding the bow and then traversing starboard. The covers were on and the storage unit at the stern was closed. With most of the portholes dark, he deduced the deck crew would be sleeping off another hard shift and wouldn't be back on the teak until six thirty to begin another day of scrub and chamois. With the fair weather and only slightly overcast skies, there would be no one on anchor watch.

Satisfied, he trod water at the stern close to the bowline that tethered the yacht's tender and listened intently. While the swim infiltration offered stealth, it suffered from the drawback that acoustics travelled far and with acute clarity across still waters at night and a keen set of ears could pick out a suspicious noise which during the day they otherwise might miss.

As he bobbed, the only sounds he heard were the slap of water against the hull and the distant thump of music from the all-night beach clubs.

Kicking forward, Shepard glided to the large swim platform, pausing at the steps to once again observe his surroundings and assess his final move before boarding the boat. At sixty-five metres long and built over five floors his climb from the water would count as less than a ripple and it was more likely a late-night fisherman might observe him leaving the water or one of the guests or crew members chance upon the intruder on a late-night stroll.

He paused another few beats, then hauled himself onto the swim deck and moved to the lee of the storage unit holding the yacht's jet skis, slides and other waterborne entertainment where he knelt and waited.

He'd spent a deal of time in the last days rehearsing what

he might say to the man responsible for the deadly double-cross that ended the lives of his colleagues, his friends, and almost his own. The mental images of Sozopol, the hotel massacre and then the short intense fight at The Palazzo Cavalieri replayed over and over in his mind. Quite why Yorke had sold out and to whom was a mystery.

With all the stops pulled out now there was a breach in operational and tactical security, authorisation and commitment from Trident's highest had been rubber-stamped and the mission to ensure Yorke could not sell any more secrets had moved forward quickly. A full spectrum surveillance package was launched, and it was Porter who had once again pulled the trump card in identifying where her former colleague had absconded to.

For the last few days, Shepard had observed the yacht personally, unwilling to have a repeat of Sozopol and what had happened with Khalid Alfredi moving safehouse.

He had sped past 'The Bella Andrea' on jet ski numerous times, spent hours under the baking sun, and cloudless nights watching the comings and goings through a high powered spotter's scope from a small sailboat moored closer to shore.

The time had come. Tonight Yorke would pay for his crimes.

Shepard bit back anger as he thought on Yorke's last days that had been full of fun and frolics, the former case officer showing no sign of remorse or guilt for what he had been part of. Instead, he'd indulged himself in booze, five-star cuisine and the occasional call girl. It could have been entitlement, arrogance or narcissism, but whatever his drive, it had, directly and indirectly, caused the deaths of too many.

Shepard exhaled slowly, lowering his heart rate for what

was to come. He was a shadow in the shadows. A spectre of death waiting patiently. Poised to deliver retribution on the traitor, David Yorke.

Chapter 21

"What shall we do with the drunken sailor? What shall we do with the drunken sailor..."

Yorke let out a belch and giggled as he stumbled on the steps leading down from the sun deck to the swim platform, a second bottle of Chianti in hand with only the dregs remaining.

He frowned as he wobbled his way across the deck, his eyes focused on the calm sea and his mind racing to catch up and match his steps across the mirage of swaying teak boards.

As he reached the edge, he suddenly felt the urge to vomit.

Twisting to grab the polished deck rail, he heaved over the side. Standing back up he then spat out to sea, wiping his mouth with the back of his hand and then swilling away the acrid taste with another slug of wine.

Vibrations trembled under his feet and he shot a glance at the deck, his face screwed up in confusion at the damp pools leading from the edge of the swim deck and as he turned, his heart leapt into his mouth as a shadow peeled away and flashed across the deck.

He dropped the bottle in shock as a hand snaked from the

blackness and gripped his larynx, forcing him back against the rails.

"Tell me you didn't quit the day job to be a cruise ship singer?" hissed Shepard.

Yorke's eyes bulged in the dull glow of the bulkhead lamps.

"One word and it will be your last. Do you understand?"

Yorke blinked rapidly, the world darkening in the periphery of his vision. He nodded furiously.

Shepard let go. Yorke fell to his knees, sucking in air.

"How did you find—"

"It doesn't matter how I found you, your problem is, I did," said Shepard.

Yorke was shaking as he fought to regain his breath.

"If you want to see the sun come up again, David, you'll pay attention and do exactly as I say."

Yorke nodded, the adrenaline clearing his head but equally making him once again feel the need to be sick.

"Toss the bottle overboard," said Shepard. Yorke complied, throwing the Chianti over the side in a pathetic overhand toss.

"Please don't kill me."

"Really, that's your best line?" Shepard took a step forward and grabbed the man by the hair.

"Did Chad Powell get that choice, or Karen Millar? Or me?"

Yorke tried to break away from the snarling operator, but Shepard had him in a vice of a grip.

"It wasn't my idea. I was following orders."

"I follow orders," said Shepard, tossing Yorke's head aside. "You're a goddam traitor."

Yorke slid across the deck to the bulkhead and cowered.

"They made me?" he snivelled.

"Who made you?" said Shepard. He stood at a right angle to Yorke and the edge of the platform, the sea lapping against the stern of the boat was the only sound as Yorke realised he had trapped himself with his answer.

"I can't tell you, they'll kill me?"

Shepard sprang forward and heaved the smaller man up from the deck.

"I'll fucking kill you, Yorke. Do you think I give two shits if you flip and spill your guts to McPeak and Porter?"

Shepard spun the man around and marched him to the edge of the deck.

"I'd rather grab that fishing gaff and ram it down your throat and let you drown in your own blood than put you on a boat to a cushy cell."

"You've no idea of what these people are capable of?"

"Do you have Alfredi's data drive?" hissed Shepard

"No."

"Where is it?"

"They took it. This afternoon."

Shepard could see the fear in his demeanour and that he was telling the truth.

"Who took it?"

"Get me somewhere safe… get me off this boat and…"

Shepard smelled the desperation and caught the glint of duplicity in Yorke's eye. It was little more than a wily attempt at self-preservation but in that instant, he saw the American buying time to plot his way out.

Shepard's self-restraint snapped, and he twisted Yorke around, clamping a hand over his mouth as he drove his arms up behind his back.

Yorke reacted violently, jerking left to right and butting his head back, but the SBS captain was physically stronger and held the dominant position, easily avoiding the wild flailing.

"You deserve a worse end than this," hissed Shepard in his ear. Yorke's body went rigid a heartbeat before Shepard propelled them both off the platform and headfirst into the sea.

As soon as the water closed over them, Yorke exploded into motion and Shepard struck long powerful kicks to drive them deeper under the waves.

His grip was as solid as a vice and Yorke did himself no favours as he fought. Any precious air he held was exhaled, flooding past Shepard's eye line in a freight train of panicked bubbles racing for the surface.

Shepard kept kicking, feeling the resistance slacken as he estimated they were fifteen, twenty, twenty-five metres down.

He felt Yorke jack-knife once, and then again a second time. His fight ebbing.

Kicking a final six beats, Shepard let his momentum slow, releasing but keeping a firm grip on his captive.

The American was still and began to drift but Shepard gave a sharp jolt to his wrist, hyperextending the joint.

There was no recoil or sign of pain. Yorke was gone.

Shepard let him go, exhaling slightly as he kicked for the surface, all the while watching the wide-eyed corpse slip deeper into his grave of cool, dark water.

Epilogue

Undisclosed CIA Facility, Vlaska, Romania.

Doctor Watson harrumphed and gave his spectacles a practised buff which he seemed to do when he needed some thinking time.

Once again, set out on the scratched and pitted table was a bibliography of Shepard's physical and mental evaluations.

"An accident?" he said, swapping lenses and then giving them a test.

Shepard shrugged.

"Disappeared without a trace?" said Watson.

"Boats are dangerous places."

"Especially with you on board?"

Shepard eased out a breath and relaxed back in his chair, choosing not to respond to the barb.

"I'm sure I heard on average almost thirty people disappear on cruises every year," said Shepard. "Without a trace." He added with a coy nod.

Watson shuffled his papers.

"You're an enigma, Captain."

"I'd disagree, sir. I think I'm an open book."

Watson chuckled and closed his notebook with a liver-spotted hand.

"Is that a challenge?"

Shepard thought about the last few days, the debriefs and the assessments and where he was going once the formality of this last interview was over.

"Sure," he said.

"Same rules apply," said Watson, giving a short cough and drawing himself up in his chair.

Shepard nodded.

"Mission?"

"Livelihood."

"Death?"

"Occupational hazard."

"Treachery?"

"Rewarded."

Watson frowned slightly at the response, scratching a note on his pad before he continued.

"Grief?"

Shepard paused, the first since Watson had begun his twisted game. He thought on the emotion.

"Raw," he said.

"Family?" Watson's tone was combative but Shepard didn't bite. He looked straight at the psychologist, aware of the eyes not just in the room, but those watching on the camera over his shoulder.

"At peace."

"Come in," Doctor Rachael McCormick's fingers skipped across the keyboard as she hurried to finish her reports and then get back into the labyrinth of financial spreadsheets, comparison analysis and qualitative data needed to complete a second presentation for her funding request.

She noticed for the first time the room was dark save the glow from her monitor and as she clicked on an angle-poise lamp, she noted on the clock the lateness of the evening.

"What's up, doc?"

McCormick rolled her eyes and pushed back her chair.

"Like I haven't heard that before," she said.

Shepard smiled as he entered her office.

"I thought I told you not to come back too soon?" she said.

He raised his hands and gave a penitent smile.

"I am on both feet."

McCormack stood up and walked around her desk, taking an edge and giving an appreciative nod.

"It's good to see you haven't undone all my hard work already."

Shepard stood midway between her and the door, halfway there but a million miles from comfort.

"Doc, look. I—"

"Rachael."

"Rachael, I wanted to say thanks."

"You did that already," she said with an arch grin. "Do I need to run another brain scan just to be on the safe side there's no sign of any residual amnesia?"

Shepard blushed, all at once at odds with the past, his future and his sudden failing attempt to communicate. He took a breath, feeling he would rather face a firing squad than tease out the question.

"Would you like to grab something to eat?"

"Like a date?" she said with a frown. "I don't know? Patient-doctor relationship." She danced a finger between them, but there was a playful light in her eyes.

"Like a thanks and a get to know you better," said Shepard, shaking his head at her teasing banter.

McCormick flicked herself off the desk, giving up on her ruse and reaching over to grab her jacket and click off her lamp.

"On one condition," she said, turning back.

"Name it?"

"You're buying because any budget I had left was blown on putting you back together."

Afterword

THANK-YOU FOR READING 'DOUBLE CROSS'

I sincerely hope you enjoyed this Mission-File. If you can **please** spare a moment to leave a review it will be very much appreciated and helps immensely in assisting others to find this, and my other books.

Continue to follow the exploits of Tom Shepard in:

'AGENT IN PLACE' and 'CODE OF SILENCE'

You can find out about these books and more in the series by signing up at my website:

www.pwjordanauthor.com

Also by Phillip Jordan

THE BELFAST CRIME SERIES

CODE OF SILENCE
THE CROSSED KEYS
NO GOING BACK

THE BELFAST CRIME CASE-FILES

BEHIND CLOSED DOORS
INTO THIN AIR

THE TASK FORCE TRIDENT MISSION FILES

AGENT IN PLACE
DOUBLE CROSS

Get Exclusive Material

GET EXCLUSIVE NEWS AND UPDATES FROM THE AUTHOR

Building a relationship with my readers is *the* best thing about writing.

Visit and join up for information on new books and deals and to find out more about my life growing up on the same streets as Tom Shepard, you will receive the exclusive e-book 'IN/FAMOUS' containing an in-depth interview and a selection of True Crime stories about the flawed but fabulous city that inspired me to write.

You can get this **for free,** by signing up at my website.

Visit at www.pwjordanauthor.com

About Phillip Jordan

ABOUT PHILLIP JORDAN

Phillip Jordan was born in Belfast, Northern Ireland and grew up in the city that holds the dubious double honour of being home to Europe's Most Bombed Hotel and scene of its largest ever bank robbery.

He had a successful career in the Security Industry for twenty years before transitioning into the Telecommunications Sector.

Aside from writing Phillip has competed in Olympic and Ironman Distance Triathlon events both Nationally and Internationally including a European Age-Group Championship and the World Police and Fire Games.

Taking the opportunity afforded by recent world events to write full-time Phillip wrote his Debut Crime Thriller, CODE OF SILENCE, finding inspiration in the dark and tragic history of Northern Ireland but also in the black humour, relentless tenacity and Craic of the people who call the fabulous but flawed City of his birth home.

Phillip now lives on the County Down coast and is currently

writing two novel series.
For more information:
www.pwjordanauthor.com
www.facebook.com/phillipjordanauthor/

Copyright

* * *

FIVE FOUR PUBLISHING

Printed in Great Britain
by Amazon